# No Time Like Forever

The Wardham Series
Book No. 6

ZOE YORK

ISBN-13: 978-1-926527-08-6
ISBN-10: 1-926527-08-9

# OTHER WORKS BY THIS AUTHOR

# DEDICATION

*some times you just need to leap*

For Elle, Kate, Melanie and Amity—
thanks for the sprints!

# CHAPTER ONE

Mari Beadie used to love bartending weekday shifts at Danny's, Wardham's only pub. She could write lyrics between the lunch rush and the after dinner rush, and the night usually wrapped up relatively early.

That enjoyment had shifted to the past tense thanks to the far too regular—and far too grumpy—occupation of the barstool furthest from the door by Wardham's prodigal son, Chase Miller.

For one thing, there was no way she could write in front of him. For another, he attracted fans. And they weren't pint-buying fans either. Often they weren't even of legal drinking age.

But right now, she'd give her eyeteeth for Mr. Grumpy Pants to be in his seat at the end of the bar. So of course he was missing, probably out back taking yet another call from his girlfriend. He'd been getting lengthy calls from her a couple of times a week lately. Mari had finally put her foot down and insisted he take those calls outside when the pub was otherwise nice and quiet. She didn't need to hear all of his private business.

That was a stupid rule to enforce, because now it left her alone with her ex-boyfriend, Joel, who really didn't understand that they'd broken up.

He leaned over the bar, his floppy dark hair landing heavily in his eyes. She wanted to yell at him to get a haircut, but he'd just twist that into evidence that she cared.

Which she didn't. At all. The man—more of a boy, really—was a useless waste of space who tricked women into thinking he was hot stuff because he had a nice voice and looked good holding an electric guitar on stage.

He certainly didn't *play* the guitar. She might have been able to forgive the stupid haircut if he could play.

"Hey, baby girl," he crooned at her. His smile was lazy and knowing. Except he didn't know—that she hated that endearment with the passion of a thousand suns, for example. Or that she worked her butt off to support herself as a musician, and there was no way she'd date anyone who took the easy way out and lived at home so he could concentrate on his art. Particularly when his art seemed exclusively devoted to getting laid and looking hot.

Mari had moved off the family farm five years earlier, when she turned nineteen, and she wasn't going to fall for another guy who lived with his parents—no exceptions. "Joel, I'm not sure why you're here. We broke up."

He tsked at her and winked. Ick. "We just had a fight, Mari. It's how we are. I forgive you." Double ick. "I want to make it up to you. We've got a gig in London next weekend and I want you to come with me. We can even get a hotel room instead of driving back."

Which he'd want her to pay for, because he didn't have a credit card. Or a job. "Not interested."

"Don't be like that." He pulled a pick out of his pocket and started playing with it. Like he even needed a pick for the basic strumming he did while he sang songs written by people with actual talent.

"Let me guess, you'd love for us to play a couple of new songs, too. And when we're on stage, me shoved to the back corner, you'll announce them as *your* new songs and take the credit for writing them. No. Thank. You."

"I wouldn't do that to my girl." He cast a baleful look at her from under his bangs, as if he couldn't remember that she'd fallen for that trick in the winter and had told him never again. It didn't matter that song had been shitty, but it was the principle of the thing—something Joel seriously didn't get. "Maybe we could write a new song together."

Yep. Didn't get at all.

"I told you, I'm not your girl. In fact…" She cast around in her head for something that would convince him to leave her alone. "I'm seeing someone else."

He just stared at her, like the possibility of her having a real boyfriend who didn't use her for his own selfish advancement was so hard to believe.

She grinned. Ah ha! "Yes. That's right. I have a boyfriend. And he has short hair." That was a stupid thing to add, but she couldn't help herself.

Joel was too stupid for her to spend time with, but he wasn't brain dead. He saw right through her. It might have been the hair comment. She cursed herself and did a mental scan of her Facebook friends list. Who could she show him on her phone that he'd buy as her new beau?

"Oh, baby girl, playing hard to get is so unattractive."

If only him thinking of her as unattractive was enough to keep him away. "I'm not playing hard to get—seriously, Joel, I don't want you to get me!"

He settled in on a barstool and tapped at the smooth wood counter. "Sure you don't. Can I have a drink while you pretend to not want to write a song together?"

No way would he pay for it, but she poured him a weak gin and tonic anyway. Then she busied herself with straightening the tray of clean glasses under the bar.

Joel kept talking about the songs they could write together. She stopped listening—paying attention to Joel wasn't good for her blood pressure. "So tell me more about this boyfriend of yours," he finally said, a little louder than necessary. Had her ignoring act gotten under his skin? Good.

She straightened up and leaned against the bar, keeping a safe distance from his grabby hands. She wasn't scared of him, just annoyed, but she still didn't want him to touch her. She closed her eyes and pictured an imaginary boyfriend. The complete opposite of Joel. Curly hair with blond highlights. Strong. Big arms, washboard stomach, no tattoos.

She liked tattoos on the right guy, but for the purposes of creating Joel's antithesis, they had to go. "He's a jock," she blurted out. "He plays all the sports. All of them. All the time."

Her ex smirked, as if to say *uh-huh*, but then his face fell.

"Everything okay, gorgeous?" The warm, rich voice rasped right behind her and she jumped what felt like six feet in the air. She spun around and slammed into a big, hard, warm, yummy-smelling chest. *Chase.* Oh sweet baby Jesus, what the hell was he doing? "Sorry I'm late. I was playing all the sports, all the time."

Mari couldn't process what was happening. It sounded like Chase was pretending to be her boyfriend. That was weird. He was also smiling. That was even weirder. He was standing really, really close to her. And he smelled amazing. "Uhm, Chase. Hi."

He crooked one eyebrow in a silent *are we gonna do this?* question. And for the life of her, she couldn't quite remember what *this* was, but she was all in. For doing anything with him, as long as he kept smiling and smelling like a surf god at the beach. When she didn't say anything else, he set his hands on her hips and turned her around. He didn't let go and she was pretty sure her insides were about to melt from joy. *What the hell was happening to her insides that they liked Chase Miller's touch?* "Mari? You going to introduce me to your friend?"

"Sure." Her voice shook, but Joel didn't seem to notice. He was staring at her very real imaginary boyfriend. "Joel Huggart, meet Chase Miller. Chase, Joel."

Chase shifted forward, keeping his left arm tightly banded around her waist, and offered his right hand to Joel. "Mari hasn't mentioned you, but then again, we haven't spent a lot of time talking about the past."

Joel took the hand, wincing as Chase squeezed a little too tightly. "We used to play together."

"Past tense?" Chase shifted his weight back on his heels, rocking Mari's body into his. Her back to his front. Wow, that felt good. She needed to put some space between them before she did something stupid like wiggle her hips like a heat-seeking missile. Mr. Grumpy Pants would soon make a return, and she didn't like him. She needed to remember that.

"Yes, past tense. Joel just popped in to say hi and then he'll be on his way, won't you?"

Her ex's face twisted in disappointment, but he nodded. Good, mission accomplished. She went to take a step away1 from Chase, but his arms tightened around her waist. She glanced back at him over her shoulder, not sure how she felt about the curious look on his face. She didn't hate it. Butterflies took flight in her stomach.

"Chase," she started to say, but after his name, her mind went blank.

"I have to…" His voice was unexpectedly gruff, and he tried again. "I actually have to go. I just wanted to see you for a minute. And I'll be back later."

"Okay," she whispered, not sure what he was doing, but it seemed like a decent way out of their charade. But then he turned her around and ever so slowly lowered his mouth to hers.

This wasn't a kiss for show. It was tentative and exploratory, like he wasn't sure he knew what to do. As if it had been a while since he'd done this. But kissing was like riding a bike, and holy crap, could Chase ride a bike. After the first few moments, commanding lust took over and he hauled her against his body. Her lips parted in invitation and he took all she was offering and more. The press of his tongue against hers made her whimper and wiggle closer, and when he pulled back she chased his face for a last little nibble of his lower lip. At some point she'd wrapped her hands around his neck and the short curls at his nape felt like magic against her fingertips.

He stared at her for a moment, and slowly she dropped back into reality. Her lips were swollen, her nipples were hard, and she'd practically begged Chase Miller to keep kissing her. She dropped her arms as her face turned red.

— —

Chase reluctantly set Mari down and stepped back.

Well, hell. The first time his dick showed spontaneous interest in a woman in more than a year and it was Mari Beadie. That was a damn shame. It didn't feel like one, but surely no good could come from getting tangled up with the woman who worked behind the only bar in Wardham. And that she was friends with his sisters…no. That had mess written all over it.

He kept his eyes on her as he moved around the bar and headed for the front door.

He'd overheard her conversation as he came back inside and decided to help her out. It was the least he could do for his favourite bartender. He'd been a pain in her side since he'd moved home—his coming to Danny's almost every day totally pissed her off. And he knew part of that was because he attracted attention, but that wasn't his fault. He didn't *want* anyone to follow him there. And they didn't stay long, not after he'd signed whatever poster or hockey puck they'd brought with them and he made it clear he wasn't up for conversation. He always stayed just a hair away from being downright rude, because that wasn't good for his brand.

Not that his brand needed to be good any longer. He was officially retired, after playing in the NHL longer than many, and he'd never had any interest in coaching or commentary. Hockey was simply a part of his past.

His present was a day filled with physiotherapy, psychotherapy and beer therapy.

And if he didn't make any breakthroughs soon in the head-game area, that would probably be the extent of his future, too.

He wasn't afraid of shrinks. Sports psychologists had helped him in his first year in the NHL, adjusting to the celebrity and the faster pace of the game—on and off the ice. So when it came up as an option after the car accident, he took it.

On the surface, anyway.

Dr. Mettner would argue that Chase was phoning in their sessions and her weekly trips to Wardham were a complete waste of his money.

He didn't care. His body was as close to repaired as it was going to get. His mind would get there, too.

And the beer therapy...well, maybe that had more to do with the pretty bartender than he'd previously considered.

Mari Beadie's ass pressed against his dick was sublime. Her ass in his hands as he kissed her? Even better.

But they couldn't do it again.

For one thing, she was way too young for him. For another, he was done with all the complications that relationships brought about. He wasn't done with women—especially not after that kiss—but he had no interest in the drama of trying to understand them all in the name of regular sex.

His mother was practically holding speed-dating sessions in her living room, trying to repair his poor broken heart.

He didn't have a broken heart.

He'd had a broken dick, but one didn't tell one's mother about those types of problems. And now that Mari may have cured him, he was free to test run his libido somewhere safe, with someone anonymous.

Not Mari.

No matter how good her ass felt.

His phone went off as he climbed into his truck. *Thank God I can finally drive this thing*, he thought. For the first six months after his accident, he hadn't been able to bear enough weight on his left leg to maneuver himself into the cab. He waited until the fourth ring to answer.

"Oscar, I'm not interested." He just sat there and waited for his friend and former agent to make the hard press. It wasn't like he had anywhere to go.

But the other man just laughed. "I stopped offering you

shit a long time ago. Nice to talk to you, too." A long, pregnant pause. "How's therapy going?"

"Great. I've started jogging." *And I'm stiff for days after. But I'm doing it.*

"That's not the therapy I mean."

"Yeah." What could he say? "Dr. Mettner's still religiously coming to my place once a week. We're talking."

"Good. Keep talking. Retirement's lonely. Listen, I'm going to be in Detroit next week. Want to come buy me lunch?"

And have Oscar see him limp into a restaurant? No thanks. "Next week is no good for me."

"Sorry, I mis-spoke. It's the week after that."

"Text me the date and I'll check my calendar."

"Maybe I'll show up at your house."

"My mom would love that."

Oscar didn't respond.

"Great talk, man." Chase hung up and slouched in his seat. He glowered at the front door of the bar until he saw Joel leave, then jammed the truck into drive and headed home.

# CHAPTER TWO

Chase didn't go back to the bar that night. Or the next day. But the day after that, he couldn't make himself stay away any longer. He sat on the beach for a long time after his morning swim, long enough for his board shorts to dry off, then he walked the three blocks to the pub.

Danny's menu was limited. French fries, wings, ten kinds of pickles and five different sandwiches. All served in plastic baskets lined with waxed paper. His last few years in the league, he'd gotten serious about his health—because the adage *garbage in, garbage out* got truer the older he got. Now it didn't matter. Besides, regardless of what he ordered, Mari would bring whatever she thought he should be eating that day. That had started some time in the spring, when she realized he wasn't going to get off her barstool and go do something useful with his life. It had pissed him off. He didn't need anyone saving him.

But he always ate the sandwiches and after a while he came to appreciate that they didn't come with a lecture. Maybe she just didn't want him to have a heart attack on her shift.

She smiled as he came in, same as always, and stuffed that notebook of hers under the counter. There were a couple of people at tables but the bar was empty, just the way he liked it. "Beer?"

He nodded. "And something for lunch."

By the time she cleared away his crumpled napkin and empty basket, the roasted turkey and cranberry chutney sandwich completely devoured, he'd figured out she wasn't going to bring up what had happened. That rankled. They were co-conspirators, so shouldn't they debrief or something? When she came to collect his basket, he slid his hand across the bar and touched her wrist. "Has he bugged you again?"

She shook her head, her dark shiny hair spilling around her shoulders. "That was great, thank you."

It really had been great. He hadn't felt the urge to kiss anyone else in the last few days, but now that she was in front of him…no. Down, boy. Terrible idea. "Glad to help."

He watched her shift away again, and chewed on the realization that despite their obvious compatibility when it came to kissing, she wasn't interested in him. Huh. Not that he wanted her to be, but he couldn't remember the last time he'd been attracted to someone and not have it reciprocated.

As if to prove his point, his phone rang. Kelly. He glanced at Mari. As expected, she rolled her eyes and pointed to the back door. It was a stupid rule, and one she didn't enforce for anyone else, but he hated these phone calls and didn't mind dealing with them in private. He stepped out into the squared-in parking and delivery area hidden behind the storefronts. "Hey, Kell. What's up?" He didn't bother to hide the sigh in his voice.

"Chase," she breathed. Everything she did was breathy and practiced. "How has your week been?"

"Fine."

"That's great." She paused for a moment, just like Oscar had. Did everyone think he needed extra time to absorb what they were saying, even when it was empty, meaningless shit? "Any further thought to coming to Phoenix for a visit?"

"No." That was a lie. There was a team event that he'd been invited to at the beginning of September that he was considering, if he could get through it without limping. Maybe coming home to Wardham had been a mistake. If he'd stayed in Phoenix, this wouldn't feel like such a monumental step. "And if I do come out there, I'm not sure that we'll see each other."

She made a disappointed coo and he rolled his eyes. Why had that ever worked on him? "I thought maybe…it's been nice, reconnecting."

"I may have given you the wrong impression, Kell. I'm still ass-deep in rehab, and with my contract up, there's not much tying me to Phoenix now." He took a deep breath. "I'm not moving back."

It felt good to say that out loud. Even though everyone knew his NHL career was over, no one talked about it. And he hadn't had to say it out loud yet. *Hadn't wanted to.* But Kelly? He could set her straight, no problem.

"I miss you, Chase." She purred his name and he waited for his traitorous dick to bounce to life. Nope, nothing.

"You miss being linked to an NHL player, Kelly. I'm sorry things didn't work out with Craig, but I'm not your guy anymore."

"I don't care about all of that. I'll come and visit you, you don't need to come here."

"Please don't do that. There's nothing left between us."

"Craig was a mistake. I never—"

That was the wrong tack for her to take. His patience wore out. "Maybe. It was definitely a mistake for me to follow you to St. Louis." He hadn't done that to her face yet, blame her for the accident. It felt good and completely wrong at the same time. There was no point living in the past, and answering her calls was just exactly that. "You know what? I'm done." He ignored the tiny gasp at the other end of the line. "If you have anything else that you need to let me know about the condo, you can go through my attorney."

That's how their stupid little conversations had started again. After eleven months of radio silence, she'd called him out of the blue at the beginning of the summer. He'd ignored the first bunch of calls, but then she sent him a text. **I have a quick question about the condo. Is this still your number?** It had seemed so reasonable. And when he warily answered the phone the next day, her question had been short and sweet, just double checking that he wouldn't mind if she had the kitchen backsplash re-tiled. Like a total ninny, he told her he preferred subway tile. What the fuck would it matter what tiles were installed in a house he never planned to return to?

His lawyer had asked him a few times already what he wanted done with his property in Arizona. In addition to the condo, which had been Kelly's before he moved in with her, but had become part his when he paid off the mortgage, there were a couple of cars and a boat. Now that he could drive stick again, he wanted his Boxster. He'd given his sister a Camaro a few years earlier, and she'd happily let him use it, but it wasn't the same.

He needed to fly to Phoenix and deal with it all once and for all. He headed back inside and ordered another beer that he nursed through an hour of reading Reddit and playing chess. Mari kept a cool, professional distance and he didn't try to talk about the kiss again. His mood hadn't improved any by the time he tapped the bar and headed back to the beach to fetch his truck.

—  —

*It won't do anyone any good if you start to crush on the local sports star.* Mari repeated the caution to herself over and over again across her shift, but she couldn't shake the searing memory of his fingers on her wrist. One touch shouldn't warm her that way. She'd played it cool, because Chase was Chase and Mari knew better.

The man practically wore a "don't poke the bear" placard. He'd moved home a year ago, and one day in the fall he'd shown up at Danny's. Head down, lips pulled tight, he'd walked slowly to the far end of the bar and taken up residence on a barstool. He'd used a cane then, but even at his slowest and thinnest, he'd still been the best looking guy in the bar.

The cane disappeared around Christmas, and by the spring, he'd packed on another twenty pounds of muscle.

Not that she'd been paying attention.

But at some point, maybe she *had* started noticing how his t-shirts stretched tight across his wide shoulders and hung loose over his tight abdominal muscles. Late spring and the end of hoodies for the year had been a secret cause for celebration in her girly bits. She'd been able to ignore the attraction because despite his good looks, he was still Mr. Grumpy Pants.

Now, though...now she'd seen a kinder side of him, in a weird *here, have my tongue in your mouth as a ruse* sort of way. But also in the slow, thoughtful looks kind of way, and when his stupid phone rang, he'd given her a shrug that said he didn't like the interruption either.

She thought about those looks and his touch as she climbed the stairs to her apartment. It was a short commute as she lived just down the street from the bar, above the sporting goods store. Worth every penny in rent, which thankfully wasn't that much. Her parents farmed not far out of town, and her brothers had all stayed at home longer, but Mari liked having her own space. She also liked that her time off was hers to do with as she wished. She'd moved out as soon as she had three months rent saved up, and had been working and supporting herself ever since.

Tending bar was a means to an end, a pretty decent means at that, and watching all sides of humanity from behind the bar usually gave her decent writing material.

Not tonight. After a quick ramen and frozen veggie bowl, eaten standing up in the kitchen because why not, she sat down with her guitar. But nothing felt right, and when she messed up her fifth chord in a row, she set her Gibson aside and glowered at it. "Stop thinking about him!" she snapped, but it wasn't her guitar's fault that Chase was in her head.

She needed chocolate. Or a boyfriend. Someone who didn't ask anything of her. She'd had enough of draining slugs. But someone who'd bring her hot chocolate and retreat quietly so she could write, waiting patiently—preferably naked—in her bed for when she needed a bedtime…story? That would be perfect.

Such a man didn't exist, of course. But if he did, Mari would be all over him like a cat on tuna.

— —

Sleep eluded Chase, but that was nothing new. He drifted in the quasi-conscious state that passed for rest, willing himself to let go. Let go of the past, and of what might have been. Of all he couldn't control.

When dawn finally rolled around, he gave up the pretence and shoved himself out of bed. He had an RMT appointment mid-morning, which meant he could run first.

And because he was a glutton for punishment, he'd swim before that.

He pulled on a dive skin, because it was his long swim day and he wasn't an idiot—the lake was cooling off in a big way as the days got shorter. Then stuffed his phone, a t-shirt, running shorts, shoes, some protein bars and a bottle of water into his smallest waterproof pack and hit the stairs. The light was on in his parents' kitchen. He wasn't in the mood for a lecture, but his mother would worry if she found out he'd gone swimming without telling anyone.

The door wasn't locked, so he let himself in. The kitchen was empty, but the steaming coffee pot flashed at him. He poured himself a half cup and drank it slowly, waiting for someone to make an appearance. When it was his dad, he breathed a sigh of relief.

"Heading out for a swim?"

"I am. You going in to open the store?"

"That I am. Your mother's in the shower. Leave her a note."

Chase swallowed a smile and did as he was told.

He followed his dad out of the house once they'd both

finished their coffees and walked across the road to the narrow strip of beach. He kicked off his flip-flops—he'd grab them when he returned at the end of his run—and waded right into the lake. He'd spent time at Erik Sorensen's beach house in Clearwater, and nothing beat an ocean swim, but the Great Lakes were still something special. Sandy shores, water as far as the eye could see, and for Lake Erie in particular, almost always calm.

His nuts pulled up tight to his body at the cold lick of water up his legs, but he ignored the internal protest and dove in as soon as he was past the sandbar. He had this routine down pat, having built up to it over the summer. Now he was swimming right into town, something he'd taken for granted in the past but had to struggle to regain this year.

He waited until he was fully warmed up before turning on the motor. The lactic acid burn felt good—he'd never take his physical ability for granted again, and proof that he was working hard just pushed him further.

The only soundtrack to his swim was the chop of the water against his face as he took breaths every few strokes. He'd silenced all the other noise in his head by the time he rounded the first bend. This was where he drifted a bit further from shore, cutting a straight line to the next rocky outcrop. Houses and fields dotted the lakeshore road, with slivers of beach access every few hundred feet, but it all faded to a familiar blur as he powered forward. His goal was further ahead—the municipal beach in Wardham.

The sun loomed large on the horizon now, faintly warming the top of his head as he swam east, and he relaxed into his new normal for training. No external goal. No competition. Just Chase versus his body. And sometimes, when it went well, it actually became something of a cooperative venture.

This morning was one of those good days. A quick glance at his watch showed him he'd done the almost 3k swim in just over an hour. *An hour and twenty minutes, no rounding down.* And it got even better as he approached the beach and saw a familiar dark head of hair bent over a notebook. Mari was sitting at a picnic table on a built-up concrete pad overlooking the west end of the beach. She was head down, concentrating on her work, and he was loath to interrupt her.

But on the other hand, a private early morning meeting on the beach was a better opportunity to talk about the spark between them than he'd ever get at the bar.

*Talk isn't quite the right word for what you want.* He wanted that feeling again, of a warm woman in his arms, reacting to him as a fully whole man. And no matter how cool Mari had been the day before, his kiss had worked for her.

But he didn't—couldn't—lead her on. His life was still too broken for dating. As Dr. Mettner told him when he finally confided in her that he hadn't been aroused since the accident, he needed to work on himself before he could give enough to be fair to a partner. He'd scoffed at the time, because after the disaster of his relationship with Kelly, he never wanted a *partner* ever again. But he *did* want to have sex again.

Mari had definitely stirred that physical awareness in him. Not just with the kiss, but yesterday again, in a way other women didn't. At his parents' store, Melody had flirted with him pretty consistently since Christmas, and *nada*. The receptionist at the physiotherapist had given her best *I'm open to being asked for my number* smile. He hadn't asked.

And here was Mari, writing away at eight in the morning on the beach, and even after more than an hour in the lake, he instantly felt a tug of awareness.

*You're not in high school, so no need to get an erection when you're just wearing a dive skin.* After a year of willing his dick to work, the mixed message was confusing, but he managed to hold his appreciation of her fine form to a simmer.

He cleared his throat as he approached, and she glanced up. He didn't miss the double take, and enjoyed the way her gaze dropped to his knees and slowly raked upward again.

"Can I join you?"

She waved at the bench opposite. "It's a free country."

Tough girl, like she hadn't just checked him out. But even when Mari threw up boundaries, she was never a bitch about it. Just…wary. Well, he could identify with that. He liked that she was prickly, albeit in a softer, gentler way than he was. He liked *her*. It was oddly unsettling and comforting at the same time. Like no matter what panned out from the spark between them, she might be a friend.

He unzipped his dive skin to his waist and opened his pack. Even though he was still damp, his t-shirt would be more comfortable than the skin, and less…douchey somehow.

"So," he said once he'd shrugged on his shirt. "What dragged you out of bed so early this morning?"

# CHAPTER THREE

Mari couldn't very well tell Chase that she'd woken up two hours earlier than usual because he'd gotten under her skin with that kiss. Not when she'd done such a good job of playing it cool the day before.

Besides, at the moment she was having trouble forming sentences of any sort, given that he'd just stripped down in front of her. The image of water rivulets running down his shoulders and between his *very* nice pecs was now burned on her retinas. Not that she was complaining. Couldn't even if she wanted to, because she'd temporarily lost the power of speech. And he hadn't even noticed, because he sat there rooting through a backpack with his wet suit pulled down to his waist. Who carried a backpack while they were swimming? And for that matter, who in Wardham went swimming at the break of dawn in a *wet suit?*

*Greek gods*, she decided. That's exactly what he looked like, with his flexing muscles and dark blond wet curls framing a face that could have been carved from marble, all lines and hard planes. Except for his lips, which she knew from up-close-and-personal research were surprisingly soft. Well, soft *and* firm. Jeez. But looking away from his face didn't help her focus, because her attention snagged on yet another water droplet, and she followed this one right down into his golden brown chest hair. Less than she'd expected, to be honest, which meant admitting to herself that she'd thought about what he looked like naked.

Thought about. Google Image searched for. It was a shame the man had never posed for something like a hockey player calendar. All she'd found were some locker room shots, but they were blurry. He just wasn't the type to often hang out in front of a camera, with or without a shirt.

"You're up early," he said again, sliding a slow glance toward her muffin. She'd stopped for breakfast at Carrie Nixon's bakery/coffee shop, Bun in the Oven, before coming to the beach. She didn't want to share, but maybe if he was eating, he wouldn't notice her ogling him. "Hungry, are we?" She jerked her eyes back to meet his gaze. *Busted.* He wasn't talking about baked goods.

"Nope, all yours." She shoved the blueberry crumble muffin across the table with a scowl, her stomach growling at her for being a fool.

He reached for it, all relaxed cool guy with a laid-back smile—a very decidedly un-Chase look—and held it up between them. "I bet we could find a way for this to satisfy us both."

She swallowed hard. Oh, shit. He was definitely flirting. This was unexpected and hard to process on an empty stomach. "You can have half of that, but I want the good part." She reached across the table and twisted the crumble-heavy top off the muffin.

Chase just watched, his laconic smile making her think of how he'd look at her in bed. On a table. Up against a wall. The cool of the morning was evaporating faster than she could say *is it getting hot in here?*

She took her muffin top and turned toward the water, where three seagulls were getting excited about the remnants of a hot dog bun. They hopped their way down the beach as they fought.

"We haven't had a chance to talk about what happened," he drawled slowly. No point in pretending he was talking about the new Wardham Community Centre—the hottest topic in town—or the weather. The only thing worth talking about between them was a super-hot kiss and how Chase had held her tight against his body long enough for it to affect them both.

She didn't turn back to face him, just shrugged and stared out across the lake. "You asked yesterday. I thanked you. Did you want something else?"

He rifled through his bag again, the rustle of nylon giving her enough of a clue about his silence that she could keep pretending she wasn't paying him any attention. He quietly shifted down his side of the table, slipping into her peripheral vision. He moved her coffee cup closer and tapped the brim with a water bottle of his own. "Cheers. Thanks for the muffin."

She took her time eating, and when she'd licked the last crumbles from her fingertips, she finally spun back in her seat to face him. "Nice wetsuit," she deadpanned.

He grinned, and she realized that for all the days he'd spent across the bar from her over the last year, she'd never seen him smile as many times as he had already this morning. She liked it, but she couldn't let herself revel in that. There was something dangerous about thinking she and Chase were the same species.

"It's a dive skin," he said blandly, and that right there was one difference. He knew all the fancy names for the expensive full body swimsuits. He probably went to the Cayman Islands and snorkeled with Brangelina on long weekends filled with supermodels and Patron.

He was a sexy-as-sin professional hockey player, recognizable by everyone in Essex County and many far beyond. He was older. More experienced, although she was no innocent girl.

In short, he was so far out of her league it wasn't funny.

And he'd kissed her, which now that she thought about it, really pissed her off. Because if everything else was different—frankly, if *anything* else was different—she'd want to do that again and again with him. Like everything else in his life, the man had more than a little kissing talent.

"Tell me about your swimming backpack."

He harrumphed, but his gazed stayed warm, like he saw right through her. "It's not...well, it is a backpack, but I

21

don't wear it on my back when I'm swimming. It floats, and it attaches to this loop on my suit."

"Fancy." But for all the expensive kit, he had a surprising lack of pretension about going for a long open water swim, trailing a bag along behind him. And the t-shirt he'd pulled on wasn't some fancy wicking sports fabric. It was a faded white cotton shirt that announced *Essex Fall Fair 1996*. "Nice shirt."

"Keep poking, Mari." The smile had slid off his face at some point, and his lips were back to the firm straight line set that she was more familiar with. But his eyes...jeez, he really needed to stop looking at her like that. Like it didn't matter how prickly she was, he still wanted to kiss her again.

And as if to acknowledge what was clearly on her mind, maybe to underline it, he looked at her mouth.

"I've got to get to work," she muttered, standing up.

"The bar doesn't open for three hours."

"I do other things." She grabbed her coffee cup and her notebook.

"Like what?" He pulled running shoes from his bag, brushed the now dry sand from his feet, and laced them on. "I'll walk with you."

She glanced at the dive skin hanging low on his waist. The hair there was darker and thicker than on his chest, and she needed him to cover it up. "You're going to walk through town like that?"

"What?" He glanced down his body. He had a good point. Somehow he made the totally ridiculous outfit look hot. His legs were nicer than hers, for Pete's sake, and they looked great wrapped in spandex. "I've got shorts in my bag, I'll get changed if you'd rather."

"I'd rather walk myself back." She crossed her arms over her chest. "It has nothing to do with what you're wearing."

"And everything to do with the fact that I kissed you the other day?"

There. It was out in the open.

She pressed her lips together. She wouldn't blush. Hot

guys kissed her all the time. It was fine. It had *not* rocked her world, and she did *not* want to do it again.

He stepped closer. Not crowding, just close enough for her to realize he wasn't wearing his usual sunscreen. He smelled like the lake and nothing else. His shirt was damp where it stretched tight across his muscles.

"Did you hate it?" he asked quietly, his tone both polite and pressing.

Her breath caught in her throat. She couldn't say yes. "You've got some talent in that area," she grudgingly admitted. "It was nice."

"Maybe we should do it again sometime." He winked, another uncharacteristic Chase move that made her think she was seeing a secret side of him. *He's just flirting. Ignore, ignore, ignore.* "Not today. But soon."

"We shouldn't," she murmured, not trusting herself to speak any louder lest her arousal make itself known.

He nodded. "Probably not. But we will."

— —

Chase's jog home was as slow as his swim had been fast. The strange comfort he'd felt sharing a muffin with Mari started to dissipate while he ran and dissolved completely by the time he finished physio.

When he pulled up to his parents' property, an acreage outside the village overlooking the lake on the way to Colchester Harbour, he just wanted to climb the stairs to his loft and lock himself away from the world. He'd helped them renovate the house a few years earlier, and had commissioned a private loft apartment to be added above the garage. It had been a great summer home when he officially lived in Phoenix. Now it was just depressing that he was thirty-three and essentially lived with his parents, even if his net worth far outstripped theirs.

But for now, it was his only refuge.

Dr. Mettner's voice vibrated in his head. *If you didn't want to live there, you wouldn't.*

Some days he was closer to moving out than others. Days like today, when he'd come back and find his sisters and his mother drinking iced tea on the wraparound porch, knowing that they'd want him to join them.

He climbed out of his truck slowly, hating the stiffness in his thigh and the fear with each step that his leg might give up as it sometimes did when he was tired. The giggling conversation he interrupted didn't resume as he sat down. His younger sister, Audrey, the baby of the family at twenty-two, had just graduated from university and was living at home for the summer before leaving in nineteen days to teach English as a second language in Japan. His older sister, Karen, had just returned to Wardham after a year in Toronto where she got her Masters of Library and Information Science degree. Newly married, Karen lived with her husband Paul and her stepdaughter Megan in the village, right next door to her old house.

*House.* Would renting from his sister be better than living over his parents' garage? He quashed that thought as quickly as it occurred to him. He wanted space, no matter what Dr. Mettner thought.

"Did you have a good swim? You headed out ages ago." His mother handed over a glass of sweetened tea.

"Yep." He turned to his sisters. "What's on the girl talk agenda today?"

Karen grinned like only a big sister could. "Uteruses."

"Oh please, it takes more than that to scare me off. What, are you finally knocked up?"

Audrey smacked him lightly on the arm. "Dude, that's so insensitive. But yes, she is."

"Yeah?" Well all right. He leaned forward and squeezed Karen's knee. "That's fantastic news. Paul must be proud of himself."

His mom laughed as Karen turned pink.

"Like a freaking rooster," she scoffed. "I'm the one growing a baby, he just had to…"

Whoa. Too much information. Audrey and Grace cackled as he pushed to his feet. "Uteruses I can handle. Your husband's sperm...I don't know."

His mom forced a sober look on her face even as her shoulders shook with silent laughter. "Was there something else you wanted to talk about, honey?"

While they were distracted by talk of babies was as good a time as any to drop a bomb. "I think it's time I start house-hunting."

"Oh." Her face fell for real and he felt like a schmuck for hurting her feelings. "You need your space—I get it."

"Yeah." He looked to Karen for support, but she was studiously inspecting the rim of her glass. Audrey had yanked out her phone, also avoiding eye contact. He searched for an explanation that she'd like. Dark, shiny hair and a safe disinterest in all things Chase Miller came immediately to mind. "Because I've started seeing someone."

Like a starter's warning at a foot race, that grabbed all of their attention. Three heads jerked his way in a synchronized swish. "You have?"

Damn. The look of hope on his mom's face was only outdone by the pure skepticism rolling off his sisters.

*Don't say her name.* "It's early days yet, but yeah."

"Not Kelly again..."

"No. Someone local."

Audrey canted her head hard to the side and bugged her eyes out at him. "Well...who is it?"

"Really? You think I'm going to unleash the three of you on some poor, unsuspecting woman? You'll meet her...soon. When we're ready." *Which might be never if a certain bartender isn't interested in returning a certain favour.*

— —

Barely forty-five minutes into Mari's shift, when she was still reeling from being eye-fucked by Chase Miller on a public beach, his sister Audrey barrelled into Danny's. For two siblings who'd become regulars at the same pub, they were never there at the same time. Audrey didn't shun the social hour the way her brother did—in fact, she'd embraced it. Wardham was a small town and anyone even remotely close in age knew each other from the bus ride into Essex for high school every day. Two years Mari's junior, Audrey had also run track and field and her other brother, Davis, had played volleyball with Travis, Mari's older brother.

And now in addition to being friends, they had the creepier connection of Mari knowing what it felt like to be plastered against Chase. *Really, really good.* And what it was like to *flirt* with him, too, which was something entirely different. The kiss had been almost accidental. This morning's interaction had been a lion stalking a gazelle. It had taken every teensy scrap of self-control not to blush in front of him earlier. When he brushed past her, she thought for sure he'd have heard her pulse pounding away a mile a minute.

It would get easier, seeing him and pretending she didn't know what his mouth tasted like. And until then she needed to practice her best poker face.

"Hey Mari, is Stella here yet?" Another lovely thing about Audrey...she'd bonded with Mari's quiet best friend, Stella Nixon. It was a shame that Audrey was leaving town for a year, but this summer had been great for Stella's social life. She'd always been close with her cousin Ian's wife, but Carrie was a decade older and had two kids and a busy job.

Audrey had brought some much needed youth and vitality to their social life. Mari often felt guilty for losing herself in her notebook. She wasn't an introvert—as a bartender, that wouldn't really work—but she thought about music twenty-four hours a day, seven days a week. She often woke up in the middle of the night to jot down lyrics or chord progression ideas.

So Mari was glad that Stella had someone fun to hang out with when she was so caught up in her own stuff.

Plus Audrey was *fun*. And right now her eyes were blazing like she had the best gossip ever. She leapt onto a stool and clapped her hands on the bar. "Guess. What."

"I can't even imagine." Mari nodded to the taps. "Want a drink?"

"Sure, half a pint of lager."

Mari set it on a coaster then leaned back and crossed her arms. "Okay, hit me. What's the exciting news?"

"My brother has a girlfriend."

Mari ignored the jealous sneer that wanted to curl up her lip. "Yeah, I know—that chick in Phoenix. She calls him like a million times a week."

"Kelly? Oh, no. Ew. Ick. They're long over, although I don't really get why he still talks to her, because that's just stupid. No, this is someone around here."

"Really?" Her chest felt annoyingly tight all of a sudden. "Good for him."

"I know! And my mom is thrilled. I don't know why she's so obsessed with him dating again, but she got all giddy when he told us. It's almost as exciting as my sister having a baby."

Mari did a double take. "Excuse me?"

Audrey smacked her forehead. "Oh, right! I have two pieces of big news."

"I kind of wondered when she wasn't drinking at the last girl's night, but wow, that's cool!" The entire town of Wardham had been rooting for Karen and Paul when they fell in love. Mari had worked their wedding at the Go West winery at New Year's Eve, a special favour to her brother who had been the head bartender that night. Plus then she got a prime seat for the sweetest nuptials ever—she'd been the one pouring the champagne for the head table.

Audrey spilled all the details she knew about the baby-to-be, then Mari had to make her way down the bar to take orders and remove empty glasses. When she glanced back, Audrey had company and really, that was for the best. *You can't be a nosy parker about who Chase is dating. It's none of your business.*

But it felt like her business in the worst way. She was mad at him. How dare he kiss her like that, even as a favour, when he was with someone else? And talk to his ex-girlfriend all the time as well?

And then this morning. *What the hell?*

Chase Miller was a dog.

# CHAPTER FOUR

How exactly did one propose a fake relationship?

Not easily, it turned out. For one thing, Mari wasn't speaking to him.

Of course, she never said a lot, but there was usually a smile. Two days had gone by and no smile in sight. She didn't even ask him what he wanted, just brought him food and assumed he'd leave enough to cover his bill.

Clearly, flirting with her had been the wrong tack, although he hadn't imagined the chemistry between them.

But it was gone now, or at least one-sided. And she wasn't hiding that notebook of hers, either. Every so often she'd pull it out and furiously scribble something. She didn't glare his way or anything, but something told him he was her muse and the lyrics were variations of *men suck*.

So at the first opportunity to talk to her, when the bar was completely empty, he approached like he imagined zookeepers might deal with spooked tigers. Carefully. He wished he had a tranquilizer gun, but drugging her was probably not the best start to dating.

Even fake dating.

She was curled over her notebook, her dark hair hanging in a curtain beside her writing hand. He waited a few feet away until she looked. She blinked at him, then lifted her brow in bland question. "Need something?"

"You." Not quite how he meant to start out, but it burst out of him. And it was the truth. *In more ways than one.* Being pinned down under her pointed gaze did strange and interesting things to his insides. Anger wasn't quite the emotion he wanted to stimulate in her, but it was something.

"Looking to expand your harem?" She snapped her notebook shut and shoved it back under the counter. "Not interested."

"You don't even know what I'm proposing." He followed her to the back of the bar. "And what do you mean, my harem?"

"I heard about your new girlfriend. And I know about your old girlfriend. Plus you kissed me. I appreciated the help at the time, but if you got the wrong idea about me, that's too bad."

She'd turned and paced toward him, and now she stared up with all the righteous fury she could muster. It was kind of cute, and fortunately misplaced.

"First," he said calmly. "My old girlfriend is very much an *ex*-girlfriend. Second, I've only kissed one person in the last little while, so I don't think that counts as a harem, although if you're offering to start one for me, I wouldn't mind."

She frowned. "What about your new girlfriend?"

He leaned forward, enjoying the way her eyes got all wide as his face approached hers. "If you're agreeable, I was thinking that might be you."

"What?"

He gave a slow shrug. "I may have invented a new relationship to get my mom off my back."

"Well, that was dumb." She scowled. "Now you need to invent a break-up."

"Why? We tricked that Joel guy. Come on. Pretend to be my girlfriend for a while. What's the harm?"

"Joel's a moron. I don't mind deceiving him because he doesn't know how to take no for an answer. Your mother is a lovely woman, a community leader, and someone I need to live near for the rest of my life. I don't want to hurt her."

"When we break up, it'll be my fault, don't worry."

"What, are you going to cheat on me?"

"No." He might be a jerk, but he was always faithful. He

stepped closer and picked up her hand, rubbing his thumb reassuringly over her knuckles. "I promise I won't make a fool of you, Mari."

She stared at their hands, and the near silent sound of breathing filled the space between them. Harder breathing than before, as his pulse picked up. Mari's hand felt damn good in his. And when she glanced up, her lips parted and her eyes bright, he didn't think about what his next move should be. He just acted, sliding closer still.

He covered her mouth with his, and that felt damn good too. Her lips were soft and sweet, and she smelled like blackberries. But the door chimed just as he deepened the kiss, his tongue sliding across hers, and she jumped back with a gasp.

"Be right with you!" she yelled, then grabbed his hand and pulled him back to the storeroom. She didn't look at him right away, just stood there with her hand over her mouth.

He decided to give her a minute.

She only needed thirty seconds.

"What the hell was that?" She swiped her pointy pink tongue over her lower lip and pushed a thick wave of brown hair back off her forehead.

Chase didn't really have a great answer for her but he knew enough about women that he'd better come up with something fast. He went with the truth. "You looked like you needed some convincing."

"In the form of your tongue in my mouth?" Speaking of tongues, hers did that darting thing again. It was very distracting. Made him want to kiss her again and this time, he wouldn't have the excuse of pretending to be her boyfriend or convincing her they had chemistry. Not a problem for him, but he'd clearly misread her. He backed up and bumped hard into the storage shelf behind him.

She growled and pulled a bag of napkins off the shelf, then pointed to a case of beer on the floor. "Carry that for me."

"Hey, what's going on? It's just a kiss. I'm sorry."

"You...that wasn't a pretend kiss."

"I think I missed a memo or something. Do you hate kissing? I thought you wanted me to kiss you. I'm a bit out of practice, but..."

She frowned again. "If I did, it wasn't because I like you."

"Don't worry, I'm pretty clear on the fact that you don't like me." Not on the surface. But deep down, there was a pull there. She watched him like he watched her. There were definitely *parts* of him she liked. "We've got chemistry, you can't deny that."

She stared at him through several long, deep breaths. "Why?"

"Well, you're pretty, and I've got that tall, brooding thing going on..."

"Chase!" She pushed against his chest, which was probably supposed to be some sort of protest, but really just proved how perfect their chemistry was. As soon as her palm slid against his t-shirt, her pupils dilated and her lips parted. He flexed his pecs under her hand, knowing he was playing dirty.

"Uhm..." She cleared her throat. "Why do you need a pretend girlfriend?"

"I don't really, it sort of slipped out. I've decided I need to find a place of my own, and my mom likes to keep me close, but she's also been trying to match me up with all the single women in Essex County. I thought after our kiss the other day, you could return the favour. I get my mom off my back, and a good excuse for wanting privacy."

"When really you just want privacy because you don't like people."

He rolled his eyes. He liked people well enough—at a quiet distance.

"How long were you thinking?"

"A month or two. Brief enough that no one will be concerned when we break up."

"Fine. But if we do this, we shouldn't do that." She nodded her head in the direction of the bar. "Not if you want me to pretend to be your girlfriend. No kissing."

He didn't like the sound of that. He'd already gotten used to kissing her. "I usually kiss my girlfriends. How would it be any different than what we did when we ditched the loser?"

"That was...an accident. A one-off, serendipitous, you-happened-to be-there type of accident."

"Where you accidentally sucked my face off and got me hard?"

She gasped. "I didn't, on either count."

He wanted to pull her close and prove she'd done it all over again, even with the huffing and puffing about this not being real, but it wasn't the time. "Okay, new agreement. The relationship is fake but the kissing is real."

She nibbled on her thumbnail for a moment, blinking up at him as she considered his proposition. He wanted to replace her thumb with his. Feel the bite of her teeth and the wet of her tongue on his skin. Finally she shook her head. "It's not going to work. Kissing's going to lead to other stuff."

"We can renegotiate at any point." He might have been slow to notice, but Mari was sexy as hell. Other stuff wouldn't be a problem for him, he was pretty sure, and that realization was invigorating.

"No, that's weird and awkward. And I think we're going to break up pretty quickly anyway. Lack of chemistry might be a good excuse."

He growled. "We have plenty of chemistry."

"Do you want to date me for real?"

"No." *Oh, shit.* First of all, he wasn't sure where that came from, because dating Mari didn't sound like the worst idea in the world. But more importantly, it probably wasn't the way to get her on board.

But instead of being offended, Mari just laughed. "Right? I feel the same way."

Well, that wasn't the answer he'd expected. He knew he wasn't quite the catch he used to be, but he wasn't chopped liver. "You don't want to date me?"

She laughed again. "What, Mr. Grumpy Pants? No, you've got a lot of shit going on that I don't want anything to do with. I don't have time for a relationship. I barely have time for my friendships. But I suppose I can be your beard as long as you promise your mom isn't going to end up hating me. Just no more kissing, okay?"

That was a lot to process, and she was right. He *did* have a lot of shit going on. That was fair. But on the other hand, Mari's mouth was hypnotic and her ass was soft and squeezable. "Tell you what. I won't kiss you. If you feel the need, though, I won't object."

"I'm not going to kiss you."

He lifted up the case of beer, knowing it was time to cut his losses. "Famous last words, angel."

—— ——

*Angel.*

This was a terrible idea. One casual nickname tossed over his shoulder and she was ready to throw her panties at him. Mari took a deep breath and followed with the napkins.

Walking behind him was dangerous. It gave her plenty of time to examine how his t-shirt stretched tight across his shoulders and how his butt looked in his shorts. She could totally see herself holding on to those bunching muscles— both sets, in alternating grabs—as he moved on top of her in bed. Or maybe back in the storage room they'd just left, up against the wall.

No kissing needed to be the rule for them. If he kept kissing her, it would definitely lead to other stuff.

He tucked the case behind the bar then picked up his phone and gave her a silent wink as he headed out the door. It occurred to her that she didn't even have his number, but it wasn't like they wouldn't see each other soon.

The rest of her shift slipped by in a haze, and when she headed out for the night, she realized she hadn't pulled out her notebook even once since he'd left.

After a quick shower, she curled up on her futon and reviewed the song she'd been working on at lunch time. She'd written a variation on the same refrain twice over. *Liar/Trickster/Smooth talking man, Thief/Bastard/Heart-breaking man.* Her eyes flicked to the stanza she'd put between them. *Don't pretend you care/when you've got another/and one in reserve.*

She believed he didn't, because if he did he wouldn't have any use for her, but Chase Miller was most certainly a smooth talking man. She needed to heed her own caution regardless of his feelings on fidelity.

His sister Karen had danced around the fact that Chase had been cheated on by his ex-girlfriend, but Mari didn't know how much of that was true, given that he kept taking her phone calls. And if there was one thing she'd learned from moving through music circles, it was that being a star, even just for a night, did weird things to people's brains. She couldn't imagine what it was like to be a big-time professional athlete. Maybe he hadn't been a good boyfriend.

Well, it didn't matter. She looked at her guitar, then past it to her computer. She didn't have time for a boyfriend. She had an album to finish writing, and an online platform to tend, like a twenty-first century digital shepherd. She picked up her phone. Twitter and Instagram first, because she could do those horizontally.

An hour later, she opened her laptop. Social media had led to email checking, which meant email writing, and now she had a quickie graphic design job to do for a promoter up north. It was a favour, so she wouldn't get paid, but it looked good for this guy to get her a slot on a side stage the following summer at the big folk festival he organized.

She wasn't formally trained in graphic stuff, but her brother Travis was. Like Gavin had gotten her into tending bar, Travis had shown her enough about Photoshop so she could do her own album artwork. And he'd handed down a MacBook he'd grown out of last Christmas, which had made her year. Now she had a decent little side gig going. It didn't help her work-life balance, but it gave her money to churn into website hosting, studio time, and a photo shoot soon, she hoped.

As she worked on the poster, her thoughts kept drifting back to Chase and their two kisses. Someone that grumpy should not kiss like a professional boyfriend. It could make a girl forget that she didn't have time to foster a relationship, and she might do something foolish like dive in headfirst when Chase was all shallow waters and jagged rocks. He was a good guy, but he'd lost his way after his car accident and didn't seem motivated at all to sort himself out.

Mari couldn't fathom that. He had so much privilege, so much opportunity, and he spent a good part of every day on a barstool at Danny's playing God-knows-what on his phone. Probably Angry Birds, NHL edition.

She didn't normally feel the need for girl talk, but this was so far outside her realm of experience that she needed a sounding board. She sent Stella an instant message.

By the time her friend arrived, Mari had decided to fudge the truth a bit. She couldn't ask Stella to lie to Audrey, and in a weird way, Mari felt that telling Stella about Chase's need for a fake girlfriend would be violating something special between them. On the other hand, lying to her best friend didn't feel great either.

"Thanks for coming over so late," Mari said as she led her friend into her living room. The apartment was an odd shape. The bedroom was barely big enough for her bed—her dresser was inside the closet—but the living room was oversized and had become their *de facto* hang out space since Stella and Audrey lived at home. As she sometimes did, Stella had brought an overnight bag with her.

"I have an early class at the studio tomorrow anyway, so it's no trouble. Besides, you rarely send up the girly bat signal, I figured it was important."

That was true. Most of the time they talked about Stella's unending and totally unrequited crush on her boss, Ty West.

Without needing to ask, Stella made her way into the kitchen and pulled the hot chocolate powder from the cupboard and set the kettle on the stove to boil. "Okay, spill."

Mari bounced in the doorway, nervous all of a sudden. Once she said it, it would be real. And it was kind of awesome as a secret fantasy. But... she took a deep breath. "Chase Miller kissed me."

Her friend's eyes got really big and she dropped the cup she'd been holding on the counter. "What?"

"Twice. And now we're sort of dating."

"What do you mean, sort of?"

*Yeah, about that.* "No. We're dating. It's just weird and new. We haven't actually been on a date yet." Would they do that? Probably not. That was okay. She didn't have time for dates. Or kisses.

"But you've kissed. Twice."

"Yeah."

"He's hot."

Mari grinned. "I know."

"But he's super grumpy. Is he like that when he's naked?"

Oh God. "We haven't done that. The naked thing."

"You should. He's hot." Stella giggled, and Mari didn't take offence. It wasn't a secret that her friend was inexperienced, and if she got a little thrill out of Mari's dilemma, that was just fine. "So what exactly is the problem?"

*I can't tell you.* "It can't go anywhere. We're at two totally different points in our lives, and he's...well, he's a celebrity and I'm a bartender."

"Is that how he describes you? Because I think you're a future celebrity and he's a washed-up has-been. I mean, if he's a jerk to you. Not while you're dating. Then he's just hot." Stella propped her hands on her slim hips and looked fierce.

Mari laughed. "I don't have any delusions about ever being famous, don't worry."

"But you've got so much talent! Maybe Chase could help you, introduce you to—"

"No." Mari shook her head. "No, no, no. I could never use him like that. It wouldn't be fair."

Stella shrugged. "Then you'll just need to use him for kissing. Is he good?"

Mari thought about the too short kiss earlier that day. He'd barely gotten past her surprised lips before they'd been interrupted, but she still got shivers thinking about how his eyes sparkled when his face was close to hers. How unexpectedly soft his scruff was, and how much she liked the way he kissed with his whole body, leaning into her and making her feel oh so desirable. He was such a curmudgeon until it was just the two of them, and then he was Don Juan.

"I guess you don't need to answer me," Stella teased, and Mari blushed. "So how did it start?"

This story she could tell truthfully, and when she finished recounting Chase's unexpected rescue from Joel the Annoyer, Stella was squealing. "Oh my gosh, that's so totally romantic."

It didn't feel romantic. Scary, addictive, tempting and totally wrong because it might be right in a whole bunch of dangerous ways, but not romantic. The thought of actually falling for Chase Miller made her want to throw up a little. Losing her heart to the most jaded man in Wardham would be a total disaster.

# CHAPTER FIVE

There was no reason to worry about falling for Chase. He was a decidedly unromantic fake boyfriend.

The next time she saw him, he was distracted and grumpy, and came and went without saying more than two words.

The time after that, he stopped on his way out, almost as an afterthought. "Hey, anything you need from me?"

She couldn't hold back a laugh. "Like what?"

He shrugged. "Information about your boyfriend?"

"Nope. I think I know everything I need to know."

— —

"You aren't dating Mari Beadie."

Chase scowled at his younger sister. "Yes, I am."

"She's my friend."

"So?"

"She would have said something to me."

"When? We just started seeing each other."

Audrey's face flushed. "We talk. And sometimes, it's about you."

"Do you mean you gossiped about me, and the woman I'm seeing didn't indulge in that? Because that sounds like a good thing to me."

"Whatever." Audrey slouched in her chair. Sometimes it was hard to remember she wasn't a teenager anymore. Other days she acted like the matriarch of the family. Today was not one of those days.

"Whatever," he sneered back at her.

"Enough," their father boomed from the far end of the table. "Chad, you should invite your friend to dinner next weekend." Hank Miller was the only person who called Chase by his given name. "I know her parents."

Of course he did. Everyone in Wardham knew everyone else. And if Mari was anyone else, he never would have dated her because this town was way too small, way too nosy for his liking.

*If you didn't like it, you'd move to a city. You'd still be living in Phoenix.* He really hated how Dr. Mettner's calm, bland voice stuck in his head like that.

"Yeah, maybe."

"Excuse me?"

"Yes, sir. Will do." And just like that, he was a seventeen-year-old boy again, terrified he'd never live up to his father's expectations.

And he hadn't.

Dinner conversation swirled around him, but Chase had lost his appetite. Not because of his sister, or his father. No, this was all on him. He needed to get out of his head. When he stepped back, he could see himself as damn lucky. Lucky to be able to walk—even run. Lucky to have money in the bank and options for his future. He didn't want any of them, but they were there. His mother should have taken a wooden spoon to the back of his head, and when he looked up, all he got instead was an understanding smile.

So instead of pushing away from the table and stomping off to his loft, he picked up the mashed potatoes and pasted on a smile. "Seconds, anyone?"

After dinner, he helped dry the dishes, then looked at a few properties his mom had bookmarked on the computer. A country place made most sense, for privacy and space, but he kept gravitating to homes in town. Walking distance to the small shopping strip.

Walking distance to the bar.

Whenever he asked Dr. Mettner about his alcohol

consumption, she pushed the question right back. No, he didn't think he had a problem. She'd nod and ask him about what else he did in the day, and why he wasn't...insert all the things that people thought he should be doing. Working. Going back to Phoenix. Skating.

He didn't have an explanation. Instead, he talked about what he did do. Physiotherapy. Swimming. Reading. And she'd just smile and nod.

*Walking distance to the beach.* That was better. Not really the whole truth, but better.

— —

The pub was slammed, strange for a Sunday night, but it was one of the last weekends of the summer. The tips would make up for the sore feet.

Mari was pouring a tray of pints when the phone rang. She hopped over and stuck the ancient handset under her ear, pinning it in place as she pulled the long cord back to the taps with her.

"Danny's."

"You sound busy."

Her heart didn't leap a little at the sound of his voice. No, it didn't. "Yep."

"What time do you get off?"

"We close at ten tonight, then I need to do some clean up. Probably ten thirty, but I'm not sure."

"Okay. See you later."

She frowned as she hung up the phone. Two hours later, she was still confused when he sauntered in after last call. Instead of taking his regular stool, he started straightening chairs.

"What are you doing?"

"Helping you."

"Why?"

"Because that's what boyfriends do?"

She looked around. They were alone. "Uhm..."

"Because that's what friends do?" He shrugged. "Don't overthink it. I actually just wanted to give you my cell phone number, but when I called you sounded swamped, so I thought it would be easier to stop by. And I'm not going to watch you sweep, that would be a dick move."

"You watch me tend bar almost every day."

"That's different."

"How?"

"I don't know. Give me that." He took the broom from her hand, and she ignored the little thrill she got at the brief, hot press of his fingers against hers.

"What were you up to tonight?" she asked as she pulled the tray from the till and started counting stacks of bills.

"Dinner at my parents'. They want you to come next weekend."

"Okay."

He finished sweeping up in companionable silence, and when she came back from locking the money up in the safe in the office, he was leaning against the bar, a piece of paper in his hand. "My number."

She took it. "Okay. I'll text you when I get home so you've got mine."

He watched her turn off the lights, then followed her through the shadows to the front door. She locked up and took a few steps down the sidewalk toward her place. He was still watching her, and it was…weird. Hot, but weird. "What?"

"Did you drive?"

"No, I just live up there." She twisted and pointed to her apartment.

"Okay. I'll walk you home."

She laughed. "You pretty much already have."

"Then let me pretty much finish the job." He gestured for her to start moving, and she did, wondering if he was watching her as she walked. Fifteen seconds later she stopped in front of her door, and he laughed. "Okay, I guess that wasn't necessary."

She looked back at him over her shoulder and winked. "That's okay, you got to play hero. Did it do nice things for your ego?"

He dropped his gaze to her mouth as his lips twitched. "Maybe."

"Good." She held up the piece of paper with his number on it. "I'll text you."

He nodded and stepped back. "Good."

She watched him head back to his truck, an odd feeling of regret growing in her chest. It wasn't until she was upstairs that she realized she was disappointed they hadn't kissed goodnight.

She went to her front window and watched his truck pull away from the curb. She sent him a quick text. **This is Mari's phone number. Use at own risk.**

He didn't respond for seven long minutes, probably the length of time it took him to drive home. **Good night, Mari's phone.**

She went to bed with a stupid smile on her face, promising herself she wouldn't be so silly the next day.

He was regular old Chase when he came in two days later for lunch, and they didn't exchange any more texts until the end of the week when he sent her an official dinner invite. **BBQ at my parents' place on Saturday or Sunday? Whichever day you aren't working.**

**Sunday?** she texted back.

**Done. I'll pick you up at 3.**

She wanted to protest that she could drive herself, but he was her pseudo-boyfriend, and something told her that Chase wanted to pull out all the stops in front of his parents. Show them he was moving on and he didn't need their meddling or whatever.

When he arrived, she was waiting on the sidewalk.

"You look nice," he said as he climbed out of his truck, his limp almost imperceptible as he approached. He looked ridiculously fine himself in cargo shorts and a light blue polo shirt. It was preppier than he usually went, and he wore the clothes with a badass edge that was sexier than she should notice.

"Thanks," she murmured as he held open the passenger side door for her.

She kept noticing all the little—and not so little—parts of Chase that were somehow different from other men. His hands were bigger, his skin more rugged. He was taller and his jaw was more defined. He'd get her door, albeit with a scowl. Joel had never done that. Neither had anyone else.

She had to keep telling herself that this wasn't real. He was good-looking because he was a Miller and he was an athlete. There was nothing special or magical about his sex appeal, and she'd seen all of his faults for a year. Just because she couldn't remember most of them right now didn't mean they didn't exist.

She couldn't let hormones scatter her common sense in the wind. There had to be a way to appreciate all of his fine attributes without going all silly fangirl every time she caught a whiff of sunscreen and man.

Chase's phone rang as they arrived at the Miller home, and he winced as he looked at the display.

"You want to take that? I can let myself inside," she offered. If it was his ex-girlfriend, she didn't want to hear any part of that conversation.

He frowned and muttered a distracted thanks as he stabbed the screen with his thumb and wandered away.

Mari smoothed her skirt and turned toward the house just in time for Audrey to come bounding out the door.

"I see my deadbeat brother has abandoned you already." Audrey looped her arm around Mari's waist. "That's okay. I made sangria."

"He got a phone call. He didn't abandon me."

"Whatever."

They were barely inside before Chase joined them. He tucked his phone away in his pocket and reached out, pulling her away from his sister. "Sorry about that," he whispered, pulling her in tight to his body.

She froze for a moment, then relaxed against him. *Right.* She was his girlfriend. She tipped her face toward his. "No problem."

"It was my ex-agent," he explained quietly.

"Everything okay?"

"Yeah, he just...he's a good friend. Just checking in."

His father came into the kitchen before she could give that much thought—like, why had she asked and why was he going to tell her anything, later or ever—and just as they got the introductions over with, Karen and Paul and their daughter Megan arrived.

Both of Chase's sisters were giving her some seriously doubting looks, even though their brother couldn't keep his hands off of her. Not that she was complaining. She had a glass of wine, a hot guy wrapped around her, and someone else was making dinner.

Hank and Chase got into a detailed conversation about the world beach volleyball circuit—Chase's younger brother Davis coached a women's team somewhere out west, Mari vaguely remembered—and when Karen nodded toward the deck, she reluctantly disentangled herself from the firm hold Chase had on her hip.

"Okay, spill," her friends said in unison as soon as she sat down.

She laughed. "Not much to say. Do you want me to spell out how great a kisser your brother is?"

"What happened to not having any time to date?" Karen leaned in. "I mean, if you've fallen in love—"

"Whoa." Mari held up her hands. This was exactly what she'd feared. "No one said anything about love. We're just hanging out."

"He doesn't look at you like you're just hanging out." Audrey crossed her arms.

"Hey, are you guys worried about *Chase?*" Mari laughed again. If only they knew. "I promise you, we're doing this all on his terms." Except for the kissing thing, although she'd been re-thinking her position on that point the last few days.

45

"He's been through a lot in the last year. We can't help but worry," Karen said, hastening to add, "and about you, too. Of course."

Mari lifted one brow. "Of course."

Her family was close, but her brothers had never intervened when she'd dated anyone. This was outside her frame of reference in a big way.

— —

Chase could see Mari through the window. He waited until his dad finished telling him about Davis's trip to Brazil, before excusing himself to join her. He told himself it was to rescue her from his sisters, although he was pretty sure she could hold her own. It didn't have anything to do with the fact that his side felt empty now that she wasn't pressed against him.

Pretending to be Mari's boyfriend was going to be fun. He'd forgotten how nice it was to have a soft woman curled into his side. And that this woman didn't want anything from him, she made him laugh, and smelled like blackberries...all of that was awesome. Especially the laughing.

He hadn't done enough of that in the last year.

And for the first time in months, he was one hundred percent enjoying himself at a Miller family dinner.

The screen door clapped behind him and his sisters both stopped talking. "Leave her alone," he chided gently. He leaned against the back of the outdoor sofa Mari was sitting on and rested one hand on her shoulder.

"It's okay," she grinned up at him. "They're just worried about you."

"Did you tell them I'm not a fragile flower?"

"Something like that."

"Good girl." He dipped his head and kissed her temple. It wasn't really cheating. When she said no kissing, she meant the kind that gave him hard-ons. This just gave him a modest chubby, so it was totally allowed.

From the way her cheeks pinked up and her chest rose and fell in a fetching manner under her sundress, she liked it. He filed that bit of information away to use at a later date, when he was tired of waiting for her to kiss him.

Pretending to be a couple and not having the physical benefits was a total waste of a good deal. He'd started to think that a few days earlier, but when Mari climbed into his truck, her skirt sliding high up her thighs, it had cemented in his brain.

His year of celibacy needed to be over, sooner than later, and he knew just the woman to help him out. She smelled good, and when she was around, he wasn't a total grump. In some ways, Mari having sex with him could be considered a public service.

# CHAPTER SIX

Chase sent Mari another goodnight text after he dropped her off the night of his parents' barbecue, and then again the next night. And the night after that. She'd given up on pretending the contact didn't make her happy. She was still resolutely *not* exploring why that might be.

When he came in for lunch on Wednesday, he squeezed her hand across the bar. He went to the stock room and got her another case of beer when she mentioned she was running low, and when she got a call about a Christmas concert she wanted to participate in, he shooed her away from the bar and covered her until she got back.

Chase Miller was being sweet, and she liked it. But it kind of creeped her out at the same time. Plus it might lead to confusing relationship shift. And it wasn't like Chase was the type of guy who'd want to talk about that. Or anything.

So when he stomped in on Thursday, back to his usual surly self, she buried the pang of longing for the perfect boyfriend material alter-Chase, and took the timely reminder that dude still had issues.

He buried himself in his phone for almost an hour, looking up long enough to glower at a random farmer who tried to buy her a drink and make sure she dodged the offer.

She rolled her eyes. She didn't need a bodyguard.

When he pushed away from the bar and stretched, his t-shirt riding high enough to show a yummy sliver of well-defined abdominal muscles, she thought he might actually leave without talking to her.

But just before he got to the door, he turned back and

leaned against the bar. "You done at seven tonight?"

She nodded.

"Want to go for a ride?"

She opened her mouth to say she was busy, that she had writing to do, but instead a breathy acceptance fluttered off her lips. "Sure, that sounds great."

As soon as he was out the door, she rolled her eyes at herself. She sounded like a freaking groupie. Ick.

But at the end of her shift, she didn't regret accepting his invitation. She didn't even know what he meant by a ride, if he drove a motorcycle or just wanted to go for a drive in his truck, but whatever he meant, she was already writing a song about it.

*Drive fast, boy/Pedal to the metal/Push it all away*

When she stepped out of the bar and found him waiting, leaning back against Karen's Camaro, his long legs encased in snug denim that made him look big and strong and far too virile for his own good…well, she had to take a deep breath and remember that he'd been grumpy earlier.

And when she finally managed to drag her hungry gaze north to his face, she realized he was staring off in the distance. Still grumpy. Her heart ached in an unfamiliar way at the look on his face.

"Hey," she said softly, stepping close to him.

He swung toward her, his expression lightening a bit. "Hey. Do you need to get changed or anything?"

"What are we doing?"

"Just a loop out into the country."

"I'm good."

He opened the door for her and she sank into the leather seat. When he got in on his own side, she flashed him a grin. "Did you steal Karen's car?"

"I promised her a week's use of my Boxster when I finally move it back here." He turned the car on, the engine rumbling, and slid into the slow evening traffic on the main street.

He had a Porsche. Of course he did. It probably smelled

even better than the Camaro, although right now the subtle scent of warm, woodsy leather was working its seductive magic on her just fine.

He headed out of town, north toward the highway, and she leaned back and just enjoyed the growl of the muscle car. When he got to the freeway, he headed east, away from the city and into the approaching night. The sunset's bright glare hit the side mirror beside Mari, and she snuck a look at Chase's profile. He looked like he still had a lot on his mind.

She leaned forward to turn down the radio, but he intercepted her hand.

"Hey!" she protested.

"Hey yourself. Driver gets to pick the music." He kept a hold of her hand and rested his fist on the stick shift.

She tried unsuccessfully to wiggle free. "I wasn't going to change it, just turn it down."

"Driver gets to decide to converse or not as well."

She laughed. "And you've decided to not?"

"Pretty much." He glanced at her for a moment and almost smiled.

At the next exit, he pulled off the highway and into a carpool parking lot, now empty. He turned the car off and looked at her.

"I didn't mean we needed to *talk* or anything like that. I was just going to…I don't know. Ask you what's up."

He shrugged.

"What's going on?"

"I need to go to Phoenix next weekend." He clenched the wheel until his knuckles turned white. She wasn't sure of the rules here. They weren't dating for real, and she'd made it clear she wasn't the kind, supportive type, but he'd sat at her bar for almost a year and scowled at the world, but never once had he unloaded his thoughts on her. And he'd been an awesome tipper, although she liked that more for what it said about his character than the actual money. He was a good guy, and in his own quiet way, had become a good friend. If he wanted to talk now, she probably owed him a few minutes. "I don't want to, and I'm sure if I paid them enough the lawyers could handle all of it, but I've got some cars there and there's a golf tournament. I'm not going to play, but it's for charity, so if I show up I can…"

She waited, but he didn't finish that sentence. After a minute, she decided to make a joke. "Pretend to like people long enough to sign some autographs?"

He didn't laugh, but he also didn't take offence. It was pretty close to the truth, actually. "It's for a good cause," he said gruffly.

"Will it be nice to see some of the other players?"

He nodded. "Yeah. There's been a lot of turnover, but I've got some solid friendships there."

"So what's the problem?" He glanced at her with a frown and she shrugged. "You're strangling the wheel there."

He took a deep breath and flexed his fingers. "It's a lot of stupid shit I've got stuck in my head."

"Maybe you should talk to someone about that." He gave her a weird look. "Not me. I don't mean *not* me, but like a professional."

He laughed. "Yeah, I know. I have a shrink. I was just surprised that you would think I *haven't* talked to someone about it."

"I don't think any of my brothers would go to a therapist." She reached over and squeezed his arm. "That's good."

"Well, it *should* be good. I found the sports psychologist really helpful when I got to the pros, but this time it's been less successful. So the trip back to Arizona is about…getting back on the horse."

They hadn't talked about any of this before—or anything else, really, other than how their fake relationship could be mutually beneficial—but Mari was suddenly struck by a worrying thought. "Are you going to play hockey again?"

That would be good. For him. Not for her. She *really* didn't want him to leave Wardham, a realization that gripped her insides with cold, clammy discomfort. *Oh shit. Way not to get attached, Beadie.*

"No. My contract is up, my leg is still fucked, and no other team is interested in me." He got a different weird look on his face and she shoved aside her selfish attachment to him.

Time to be a good friend, because that's all they were. Friends. "What would it take, if you wanted to play again?"

"A year, maybe more, of intensive practice and physiotherapy. More than I'm doing now." As far as she knew, he worked out almost every single day. *More* sounded daunting. "And it wouldn't be an NHL team that would take me. If I wanted to play—and part of me always will—it would be in Europe. And I'm done living an airplane ride away from my family. Plus my age is a problem. I had a good career, but it wasn't spectacular, and now I'm another year older. It's time to let the dream go."

"Bummer."

"Yeah." He let out a heavy sigh. "Hockey was my life. My entire life. That's...the adjustment has been hard."

"What makes you happy now?"

"I don't know. I really liked going for this drive." He looked at her, his eyes dark. "I really like going to the beach in the morning and eating your sandwiches at lunch time."

She pursed her lips.

"You don't approve."

She shrugged. "I haven't been through everything you've had thrown at you."

He snorted. "I'll never complain about my life. I'm a lucky asshole. But I'm at the end of a career. Moving on to something new isn't that easy for me."

She hadn't thought about it like that. "Do you want to do something else...I mean, eventually?"

"I left home when I was sixteen. Moved to Peterborough for juniors, lived there during the school year, and had camps all summer. I know it seems like I was just playing hockey, but it feels like I've been working non-stop at that for a lifetime. Twenty-five years in competitive hockey.

Almost three decades of being groomed for the NHL."

"You didn't want to play?"

"Yeah, I did. I love hockey. But I'm tired. And it's not the game…fuck, I love *hockey*. But it's all the rest that's exhausting. Someone in the public affairs office set up my Twitter account. I don't even like press conferences. I'm one of those guys who gives the same sound clip every single time."

"So?"

"So it's not good enough."

"Says who?"

He smirked, but it wasn't rude, just flippant in a self-protective kind of way. "Are you always this challenging?"

"Hey, you started talking." She smiled. "Can I drive home?"

"Nope." He slid the car into gear and tore out of the gravel lot.

Chase rolled down the windows for the ride home, and as they chased the last rays of the sunset, Mari didn't mind the lack of conversation.

When he parked in front of her apartment, he hopped out of the car and was halfway to her door before she had it open.

"You couldn't wait for me to get it?"

He leaned against the car, almost boxing her in to the vee of the open door. *Almost*. She could squeeze past him if she wanted to, but she didn't. Pretend-dating Chase was starting to feel a little real, in a flirty, fun kind of way, and she liked it.

She crossed her arms and flipped her hair over her shoulder. "Has anyone ever told you that you have some disturbing Neanderthal tendencies?"

"You don't like chivalry?"

"I don't know. There's something disingenuous about it, don't you think? You're in a bad mood. Why should you have to open the door for me?"

"I'm not in a bad mood anymore." He leaned closer and

brushed an errant strand of hair off her cheek, tucking it behind her ear. "Maybe I'm grateful for the company."

Between his thumb on her cheek and his words floating through her now thrumming blood stream, he was very convincing.

"I might want a bit more of your company, actually." His voice rumbled in the night air and she shivered despite the late summer warmth.

"I don't know if that's a good idea…" she whispered, which was a total lie. 99% of her thought it was a great idea. The remaining sliver of her conscience was wavering on the line, too.

He frowned. "Hear me out."

"Okay." She licked her lips. *Convince me, I promise it won't take much.*

"I know that you weren't sure about this when I asked you to play my girlfriend, but we've fallen into a good routine here, you know? No strings, no expectations…this is the best relationship I've ever had, Mari. None of the drama of really getting involved."

Hmmm. She didn't know how she felt about his opening line, but maybe he was warming up to the good stuff.

He smiled down at her. "I think we've become good friends, right?"

Yes. Friends. That's exactly what they were. Flirty friends, because he was an over-sexed sports god who probably didn't know how to talk to women without turning it on, but just friends. She smiled back, hoping it stretched all the way to her eyes. "Of course."

"So I think it would be great, if you could swing it, if you came to Phoenix with me."

— —

"Say what?"

Chase rolled back his words in his head. No, he was pretty sure he'd been clear, but Mari was practically scowling at him. So much for thinking they were on the same page. "Look, if it's too much to ask…"

She took a deep breath and puffed out her cheeks. "No, it's not. Okay, start over again. You want me to go to Phoenix with you? For how long?"

"Just the weekend. I haven't booked my flight yet, but probably Thursday night to Sunday night."

"Why?"

Because she settled him. If he went alone, he'd be on edge for four days straight. If she came, he could at least smell her hair whenever things got a bit much. And if she stopped scowling at him, maybe even hold her close. That would probably lead to him being distracted by the possibility of kissing her, which was a good thing, because then he'd forgot all the other shit in his life that dwelled heavily on his mind the rest of the time.

He couldn't very well tell her all of that. "Because I could use a friend."

Her face softened and she leaned in and gave him a brief hug. "Okay. I'll let you know tomorrow if I can get the time off."

The temptation to kiss her forehead again was strong, but something told him it wouldn't go over well tonight. Maybe he shouldn't have talked to her about all that heavy shit on the drive.

Maybe he should take his own advice and not over think things. He took a deep breath and squeezed her shoulder as he stepped back. "You'll text me?"

"I will." She walked slowly to her door, chewing her lip the whole way.

"I'll see you tomorrow." It didn't feel like the right thing to say. "Do you want to do something after work?" That felt better.

But she shook her head, her hair waving like liquid ink around her face. "I've got a lot of stuff to do, sorry. I'll let you know about Phoenix, okay?"

He waited outside on the sidewalk until her apartment lit

up, then he headed to his sister's place to return the Camaro.

When he walked out of the garage tucked behind their house, his brother-in-law, Paul, was sitting on the back deck. He had two bottles of beer in his hand, and he held one out for Chase.

"Thanks, man." Chase nodded to the house. "Karen asleep?"

"Yep. Pregnancy does that to a woman."

Paul would know—this was his second go round at the dad-to-be thing. Chase wouldn't have the foggiest idea. He'd never even got close to marriage, not even with Kelly, and he lived with the woman for a year. "Well, tell her thanks for the use of the car."

Paul lifted his brow in acknowledgement and tipped his beer back. One of the many things Chase liked about his brother-in-law—he was a man of few words.

They drank in companionable silence, and Paul didn't say anything until Chase stood up to leave.

"What's going on with you and Mari?"

Chase swung around, surprised that he was getting this question from Paul of all people. "Why do you ask?"

Paul shrugged. "Before you came home, before I was with your sister, I spent my fair share of nights sitting at her bar. I work with her best friend. I know enough about Mari to know she's a driven young woman."

Chase frowned. "So?"

"Emphasis on young, I guess." Paul made a face and stepped back. "Look, I shouldn't have said anything. You're both adults."

"I'm not...we're not like you and Karen. It's not serious."

"If you hurt her..."

"She has three brothers, but you can join the blanket party if you want. I'm not going to hurt her. We're just having fun." Chase scrubbed his hand through his hair. "I like her. She makes me happy. But we're not...Come on, man, we're not even sleeping together. I'm not going to hurt her."

"That was a lot of words to say one thing." Paul frowned. "And no sex?"

"Nah." Not that he didn't want to. She'd taken up a permanent spot in his nocturnal fantasies. His hard-on had zero problems working these days. "You don't need to tell Karen that."

Paul laughed. "Your sister and I don't talk about your sex life, or lack thereof."

"Thanks again for the car."

Paul quirked his lips. "Thanks in advance for letting us borrow the Porsche."

Chase held out his hand and Paul gave him a slapping shake. Chase ambled down the driveway to the street, where he'd parked his truck.

At home, he did his stretches and evening exercises, then popped *Band of Brothers* into the DVD player and lay down on his couch. His thoughts immediately drifted to Mari. *No sex*. Yeah. Maybe they'd have a chance to renegotiate in Phoenix.

# CHAPTER SEVEN

Mari had gone back and forth about the trip more times than she could count, and was still surprised to find herself sitting next to Chase on an airplane.

The intervening week had flown by, and other than a few brief conversations about the trip, they hadn't hung out.

Her frustration at realizing she wanted Chase more than she'd planned had been excellent writing fodder, however. "Special" had come together really nicely, and she'd posted a video to YouTube of her playing it on her acoustic. Since her mother, her brother and Stella were the only people subscribed to her channel, no one else would see it unless she pushed it out there onto social media, but it still felt great to have one of the new songs finalized. One down, eleven to go. She'd written songs before, but this album was going to have a different voice. A better, stronger voice, based on everything she'd learned in the last year. *And the last two weeks.*

Maybe her period was going to come a bit early or something. She couldn't think of any other acceptable reason for her sudden moodiness when it came to Chase. But she'd take the hormone roller coaster if she kept writing as well as she had been.

"Penny for your thoughts," he murmured, touching her arm.

*Ha. Not likely.* "Just wondering if it really is a dry heat, as promised."

"You weren't thinking about how much fun it'll be to spend four nights with me in a hotel room?"

"You promised a two-bedroom suite!" She jerked her head just in time to see his solid face dissolve into laugh lines and dimples. He'd shaved, and she still couldn't quite process seeing all of his face unobscured by a day or three of scruff. "When did you turn into such a jester, Miller?"

"When did you start last naming me, Beadie?"

"When you decided to turn on the charm. It violates the spirit of our agreement." She caught her tone just before it tipped out of playful territory. "Don't let it get you down. I don't let just anyone last name *me*."

"Then I'll call you Beadie with pleasure." He winked on the last word, and something primal inside her growled.

"Pretend pleasure," she whispered.

"Our agreement doesn't say anything about not enjoying ourselves. Just no kissing," he returned, mimicking her hushed tone. "Why do you object so strongly to me being nice?"

*Because I can keep Mr. Grumpy Pants in a corner. Sexy Chase can't be constrained.* "It's weird."

This time his laugh shook his entire body. "Yeah," he admitted after a minute, his words still vibrating with humour. "I guess it is."

Once they landed, Chase navigated her easily through the airport to collect their luggage. While they waited, he checked his messages. She did the same, grateful for his suggestion that she get an American data plan for the trip.

After grabbing their bags, Chase pressed his hand into the small of her back and they headed out into the sunshine. She expected him to flag a taxi or have an airport limo waiting, but instead he looked left, then right, and started off toward a man waiting at the end of the row of cars...next to a Porsche Boxster.

"Mr. Miller," the suited man said with a small nod. He held out a set of keys. "She's all yours."

"Thanks, Wayne. I'd offer you a ride, but..." Chase grinned at Mari. "I've got an important passenger with me today."

She snickered as he tucked their suitcases into the small backseat, but her smirk faded as she settled in her seat. It really *was* a nice car. She slid her hand over the centre console and wrapped her fingers around the gearshift.

"I like the look of your hand around my stick, Beadie." He lifted his brow in bland denial as she parted her lips to snap back at him, but the way his eyes sparkled, that was a waste of effort. And now he'd gone and made the last name thing sexy too.

"This is a surprise."

Chase shrugged as he eased into traffic, expertly navigating them away from the airport. "Wayne has a car storage service. The airport delivery is something he does for his favourite clients."

"And you wanted to impress me?" Even as she said it, she knew it was wrong, and she flushed hot with embarrassment. "God, I'm sorry. You just wanted to drive your own car. Duh."

He reached across the console and squeezed her arm. "No…you're not wrong. Not you, though. Nothing I do will impress you." He winked. "But I do have some impressing to do this weekend. Maybe the other guys. Maybe myself. I don't want to show up at the hotel in a rented Ford Taurus."

"Well, this is definitely better than a Taurus."

He shrugged and returned his full attention to the road.

He'd told her they were staying at the Four Seasons near the course hosting the golf tournament. She didn't quite appreciate just how nice their digs would be until they pulled up in front of it. Before she could get too excited, though, a bouncy young blonde woman recognized Chase and practically skipped over. He seemed to recognize her as well, but with less enthusiasm.

The blonde gave them a welcome spiel, then he introduced her to Mari as Cadence, one of the tournament organizers. While they were talking, Chase tugged Mari into his side, just for a second, and despite herself, she rubbed her hand up and down his spine.

That was just the warm-up. In the lobby were two players, Erik Sorensen and Ryan Dubois, Mari learned as Chase introduced them. Big, confident men in nice suits, with easy grins for Chase. Hand slapping and back thumping started the conversation, but it didn't take long for Chase to wrap his arm around Mari again, like she was his security blanket.

She was suddenly glad she'd dressed up for the flight, and let Stella convince her to borrow some clothes from her boss, Evie Calhoun. The slightly older woman lived in yoga pants most of the time, but it turned out she had a secret love of *nice things*, and her closet vomited out three perfect outfits for Mari's trip, including the linen capris and pale blue silk shell she was wearing now. She didn't miss the appreciative look Erik slid her way, and neither did Chase. He tightened his grip on her waist and took the next conversational out he was given.

"We'll see you guys at dinner. Looking forward to it." He steered her to the reception desk, his hand never straying from her waist.

"That wasn't polite," she murmured as they followed the bellhop through the resort to their *casita*. Like the valet when they got out of the car, Chase tipped him discreetly and with complete ease.

She kept noticing all the ways he'd shifted since they left Wardham. In his dark jeans and buttoned down white shirt, he wasn't as dressed up as his former teammates, but the leather belt and shoes weren't like anything he wore at home. Neither were the shirt and jeans for that matter. The outfit, the mannerisms…this was a different Chase.

The look in his eyes was different, too. "I can be a bit of a jerk," he shrugged.

"That hasn't actually been my experience. A grump, yeah, but not a jerk." She looked around their suite, which she realized took up the entire bungalow. Exposed beams and modern furnishings were an interesting mix, but as it was already the fanciest place she'd ever stayed, she wasn't complaining. "This is…wow."

"Do you like it?" Chase looked in one bedroom, then the other. "They're both kings, you can take your pick."

She followed him into one and let out a gasp. Out the patio door was a small pool. "This is amazing! I can't believe you were able to book it at such short notice!"

He made a face. "It took some finagling. I had to ask around, because regular rooms were all that were available. Tommy Laval had this suite for his family. I told him I had a new girlfriend to impress, and he was happy to switch."

"He didn't think the extra bedroom was a bit unnecessary for you and your new *girlfriend*?"

"I'm sure he didn't even think about it. I offered to take his spot in the tournament on Saturday so he could spend the day with his kids instead."

"You'll be golfing? That sounds dangerously social." She twirled on the spot, then skipped to the bathroom.

"*We* will be golfing, actually. It's a foursome, and Tommy and his wife were both signed up."

She dashed back into the bedroom. "Oh, no. Chase, I've never golfed before." She didn't even think she had anything appropriate to wear. "Why didn't you tell me this before we left?"

"Because you seemed sort of on the edge about coming or not, and I figured it's better to beg forgiveness." He grinned. "Besides, I'll have a lot of fun teaching you."

"I'm going to need to do some shopping tomorrow."

"I'm heading into the city. Do you want to come with me?"

"I'm sure I'll be able to find something here." It would probably make her credit card weep, but he'd flown her to a four star resort in Arizona so he could hold her close from time to time. Buying a new outfit wasn't that big a deal. She pushed that thought away and put on a no-big-deal air. "That will maximize my poolside time."

That Different Chase look made an appearance on his face again. "Good motivation for me not to waste the entire day at my lawyer's office."

He wanted to see her in a bathing suit. *Oh boy.* Or maybe go swimming himself, she told herself, but she wasn't an idiot. He raked a hot glance down her body and back up again. Yeah, he was picturing her in a bikini right now. He'd be sorely disappointed when he discovered she'd only brought one-piece swimsuits.

*You could add something skimpy to your shopping list*, the devil on her shoulder said, but she shuddered at the thought of how much a bikini would cost in the gift shop. No, a golf outfit was more than enough.

"Remind me again what our itinerary is for the weekend?" *When do you need me to play the adoring girlfriend?*

He relaxed against the doorframe and slid his hands into his pockets. "Drinks with the guys tonight—you can skip that. Alumni reception tomorrow night, which I'd appreciate you coming to. Golf on Saturday…" He smirked at the probably unimpressed expression on her face. "And then whatever you want to do on Sunday before we fly home."

She bit her lip, hesitating because she was worried the only thing she wanted to do would make him uncomfortable. "I want to hike Pinnacle Peak one morning, before it gets too hot."

As she expected, his lips tightened and he dropped his gaze. "Do you want me to find someone to go with you?"

"No, I'll join a group. I read online that there's a guide-led tour almost every morning."

"Because I can't—it's not the walking, but—"

"I get it." If they were in Wardham, he'd climb the bluffs and deal with the fallout if his leg gave out. She'd seen him run and swim on the beach enough to know he was physically capable…most of the time. But if he had to get medical aid to transport him back to the resort, where many of his former teammates were staying for the weekend…he couldn't risk that embarrassment.

"It's gorgeous," he said gruffly. "I've been up there a few times. You'll like it."

"You'll keep the hot tub warm for me?"

"You bet." He shoved off the wall and muttered something about unpacking. She decided to do the same and followed him back to the living room, but by the time she got to their pile of suitcases he'd disappeared into the other bedroom and closed his door.

She hung her clothes in the wardrobe, then changed into one of the two swimsuits she brought, then slipped through the door that connected her bedroom to the private patio and the pool. She couldn't worry about Chase's mercurial moods when she had a plunge pool at her disposal. And he'd snap out of it on his own.

— —

Chase took off his clothes and draped them over the back of the chair in his room. After the flight, he needed to do some exercises to keep his leg limber.

He'd been physically active his entire life, and fitness had been something he'd somewhat taken for granted. It had been hard work when he looked back at it, but he'd always stayed on top of it with the conditioning programs dictated by the team. The irony that it took a career-ending car accident to make him truly appreciate the fragility of his physical strength wasn't lost on him. No matter how many stretches, lunges, lifts, sit-ups or planks he did, he'd never regain full feeling in his leg, and the muscles might always be unpredictable like they'd been in the last few months.

And if he didn't…the thought of his leg getting worse had him push through the aggravation of not being whole, because nothing was going to change that, and he was damn sure he didn't want to get any weaker than he already was.

In just his boxer briefs, he pushed himself the memorized Thursday routine, then jumped into the shower for a quick rinse off before pulling on his board shorts.

Just as he put his hand on the slider door, Mari got out of the pool. Like a magnet, his cock rose in his shorts, pointing straight at her gorgeous curves wrapped in slick black spandex. One of the straps on her one-piece suit slipped off her shoulder, revealing a slice of side-boob that made his nuts ache.

*She's too young, too nice, too uninterested.* But every time they kissed she was all the way in.

The memory of holding her against him, of licking his way into her mouth and feeling her give in to the chemistry between them…that made him want to jerk off in the worst way. But she was heading inside, and he wasn't that guy. He wouldn't risk making her feel uncomfortable if she heard something.

And thinking of Mari, he couldn't guarantee he'd be silent. He let out a slow, controlled breath and stared up at the ceiling. *Don't think of her on her knees. On all fours. Standing over you on the bed, legs parted just enough to see how wet…*

Knock. Knock, knock.

He whipped around and glared at the door. *That's why you don't jerk off while she's in the suite, numb nuts.* "Yeah?"

She paused for a minute. "Uhm, we didn't discuss dinner," she called through the still closed door.

He shifted his glare to his heavy erection, still straining against the flimsy fabric of his shorts, then stepped to the door, cracking it just enough to talk. His upper body was bare, so he waved his hand. "Sorry, just changing."

She turned pink, all the way down her neck to the V of the black t-shirt dress she'd put on over her suit. "My bad."

"No worries. Do you want to order room service? Or go to the restaurant?"

"Oh." She nibbled her lower lip like she did when she was unsure, and he wanted to pull her close, but so did his cock, so that was a bad idea. He kept the door firmly between them. "Maybe we should just order a pizza? Or go and grab something?"

*Damn.* He clearly hadn't done a good job of communicating that this whole trip was on him. "I'd kill for a steak. Let me throw on a t-shirt, then I'll call and place an order."

He found her in the living room a few minutes later, looking at the menu and chewing on her thumb. "What's wrong?"

She winced. "You're going to think I'm silly."

"Never." He sat on the same couch as her, a seat and a half away. *Like that safety zone would matter if she gave him the right sign.* But she wouldn't.

"It's just...I don't need something fancy for dinner. Part of me just wants to order a salad. This thing doesn't even have prices on it!"

"Okay." He shrugged. "That's not silly."

"No, the silly part is that I'm starving, and I want a hell of a lot more than salad."

He tipped his head back and laughed. "Give me that." She sheepishly handed over the menu and he reached for the phone. He ordered one of almost everything. When he hung up, she was staring at him with her mouth hanging open. "What? I'm hungry, too. They said it'll be about an hour—will you survive until then?"

She stood. "Okay, I'll shower and put on something with an elastic waistband."

He laughed again and watched as she bounced off to her room. His phone chirped and he read the text message from Tommy. **Heading to the restaurant with my wife and Danny-boy. Want to join us?**

**Sorry, man. We're eating in tonight. I'll see you at the bar later.**

**Take your time. ;)**

He would, even though it wasn't like that.

— —

Mari heard their dinner arrive as she smoothed moisturizer down her legs. The shower had turned into a longer-than-anticipated bath. She pulled on a pair of stretchy cotton shorts because Chase had ordered a ridiculous amount of food, and a tank top because there was nothing that could dress up cotton shorts. When she stepped back into the living room, she was glad she hadn't put on a dress, because Chase was still in his board shorts and t-shirt.

But their feast was laid out at the dining room table, complete with roses and lit candles.

"This wasn't me," Chase blurted out faster than she could say *nice table setting.*

"Okay…" She dragged out the word. "I wouldn't have assumed anything if it was."

"Should I take that back?" He winced. "Is this totally your thing and I've just ruined dinner?"

She grinned. "No, steak and lobster is totally my thing. How they're dressed up doesn't matter to me."

"Good," he said, pulling out her chair. "Let's eat."

He poured her a glass of red wine before he sat on the opposite side of the table.

She surveyed the seven dishes spread out between them. "I think we'll have leftovers for lunch tomorrow."

"Or a midnight snack." He winked, and a single butterfly took flight in her stomach. Candlelight did obscene things to Chase's eyes. Filled them with dirty promises that ensured she'd wake up in the middle of the night, all hot and bothered.

Oh well, at least she'd have something to munch on while she clenched her thighs together and pretended she didn't want to jump her fake boyfriend.

# CHAPTER EIGHT

Mari was asleep, her door shut and the lights all turned off, when Chase got back from the bar that night.

He grabbed some leftovers—Wagyu short rib ravioli—and climbed into bed, flipping on the TV to catch the late night news. He lasted all of seven minutes, until the sportscaster mentioned his name.

*Nope, not ready yet.*

How freaked out would Mari be if he curled up in her bed to sniff her hair? He laughed to himself, but it was only partially a joke. He'd been playing it pretty cool, but he'd have had trouble walking into the lobby without her earlier. And she'd worried about the cost of dinner. *Jesus.* He owed her the moon.

Dinner had been fantastic. They'd dug in and the conversation had ebbed and flowed in a natural way. If she hadn't started yawning, he would have blown off going to the bar, but he was glad he tore himself away from her. For one thing, drinks with the guys had been nice. Low-key, which was probably Tommy's doing, and the hockey talk was about *hockey*, which he never stopped loving. It was nice to be back in the thick of that for a couple of days.

It was also good that Mari didn't give him any openings to make things physical. They had a whole weekend together. He wasn't sure she'd reciprocate his interest, and if she didn't, it would be damn awkward sharing a suite with her. He could take rejection like a man, but there was a time and a place to be told no and tonight wasn't it.

Maybe tomorrow, if he caught her swimming again.

But when he woke up, she was gone. She left a note explaining that the concierge had alerted her to a group heading to the Peak and she'd be back for a late breakfast.

*By which time I'll be in the city.* He knew he wouldn't get to spend the whole time with her, but after dinner the night before, he'd been looking forward to ordering room service for breakfast. One of everything, with a side of more laughter than he deserved.

He scrawled a response—**back in time for a late lunch, be hungry**—and went reluctantly in search of a suit.

— —

Mari ate leftover roasted vegetables and Chilean sea bass when she got back, which made for an unorthodox but truly delicious breakfast, then took a shower and crawled into bed for a well-deserved midmorning nap.

The next thing she knew, Chase was standing in her doorway, backlit by the natural light streaming into the living room, and he was wearing a suit. She was pretty sure she had to be dreaming, which made the fact that she was naked under her sheet totally fine.

"You getting up?" he rumbled, and she let her eyes drift closed again.

"Mmm-hmm."

"You want some coffee? I ordered way too much food again."

She froze. The sexy vision in a suit, all tall and broad...that wasn't Fantasy Chase.

"Uhm," she said, her voice wavering. She kept her eyes closed, because if she couldn't see him, maybe he couldn't see her. Naked. Under nothing but a thin white sheet. Well, it wasn't that thin. Thank god for high quality linens, Four Seasons.

"Come on," he cajoled, and then all of a sudden he was moving closer. "Here—"

"No!" she half squeaked, half yelled. "Out!"

"What?"

"Chase! Get out of my room." She burrowed deeper under the sheet, shifting her toes around looking for the blanket that she must have kicked off in her sleep.

A long, heavy pause filled the room. "Mari…" He left her name hanging in the air for a long, knowing minute. "Are you naked?"

"Out."

"Because if you want lunch served in bed…"

"Out."

"I'm happy to oblige." He laughed as he stepped back, then closed the door. She cracked one eyelid open, peering this way and that, double checking that in fact he was gone before she slid off the bed, pulling the sheet with her as she scurried for the wardrobe. *Sleeping naked, what the hell were you thinking?*

Well, now that she *was* thinking, lunch in bed, served by Chase, sounded pretty nice.

*No.* There was no point arguing with the inner independent woman that had no time for men. She'd just throat punch any other part of Mari that wanted to get wound around the axle for Chase.

She pulled on yoga pants, a basic bra and underwear, and a dark blue t-shirt. Covered from collarbone to kneecaps in boring dark colours. *A bit clingy, don't you think?* She growled at herself. So he noticed she was naked. It wasn't like he actually saw anything other than her shoulders.

And when she stepped into the living room, his lips twitched but he didn't say anything. He was a hot-blooded man. She already knew that. He'd teased her a bit, but that would be the end of it.

"You said something about coffee?" she muttered, focusing on the table.

He slid the mug he'd already prepared for her into her hand, then busied himself with filling a plate. Tomato salad, grilled fish. The most amazing sandwiches she'd ever seen.

"You really did order one of everything," she said,

swallowing hard.

"I skipped the soups."

"Good call." She ate a few bites, then set down her fork. "You aren't usually this wasteful with food, are you?"

He wrinkled his brow at her. "No. And it's not wasteful if we eat it all."

"I'm not sure that would be healthy."

"We're on vacation. I've never been able to just kick back and be a glutton before, and I've had no reason in the last year. Humour me."

"Live a little?"

He nodded. "It's possible I haven't been doing enough of that."

"You think?" She pressed her lips together. More eating, less blurting out judgemental statements.

But Chase didn't seem offended. He just shrugged and pointed his fork in her direction. "What keeps you so focused?"

"What do you mean?"

"Your songs. It's not a casual thing, your music."

Her first instinct whenever this came up—with her parents, her brothers…everyone but Stella, really—was to play it down. But Chase might understand. He'd done the impossible, a Wardham boy making it to the NHL. Maybe he wouldn't think her optimism was pie-in-the-sky. "No. I've been saving up for studio time."

"How close are you?" He leaned forward and rested his elbows on the table.

"I've got the money. But the songs I wrote before don't feel like an album, so I'm working on some new stuff. I should be ready to record in November."

"I look forward to hearing it." He held her gaze. "Can I be of any assistance? Do you need an investor?"

She grinned. "No, but thank you. If I do it on my own, then I get to reap all the rewards."

"This is why you aren't interested in a relationship right now."

Had she said that? Such an easy statement to make before she'd spent time in close proximity to him. "I don't want to be distracted. Or maybe I worry that I'm easily distractible."

"Maybe all you need is someone who gets what it's like to be focused on an impossible dream." He held up his hand. "Scratch that. A possible dream."

Lunch lay forgotten between them, and she felt the tug. She could follow him down that path, see what giving in to the attraction between them would feel like—probably pretty amazing—but she was scared. So she played dumb. "Was it worth it? All that work for your career?"

"Because it ended a bit early?"

She nodded, and he looked away, staring off through the patio door to the bright Arizona afternoon sunshine. "Yes. I wish I'd achieved more, but I can't regret what I had."

"Do you ever think about the path not taken?"

He shook his head. "Never."

A heavy knot lodged itself high in her chest. Maybe that was the difference between Chase and her. At her age, he wasn't saving up for his first hockey stick, he would have already been in the NHL. Maybe she was just playing at being a songwriter, and deep down she was too fascinated by the alternative. Finding a job, having a social life, just *living* the way Stella and Aubrey did.

He reached across the table and grabbed a cherry tomato from the bowl in front of her. He'd taken his suit jacket off and rolled up his shirtsleeves, and the dark blond hair on his forearm grabbed her attention. He was the golden boy on every level. Sun-kissed skin covered by bronze-tinted hair. She tracked his hand as he carried the tomato up to his firm lips. He held it there for a minute, and she flicked her eyes up to catch his gaze.

"Tell me more about the path you're not taking," he said quietly.

"Fun, I guess."

"Don't you play with rock bands?"

She wrinkled her nose. "That's *not* my definition of fun. The music is great, the sketchy clubs and drugged out guys are not."

"Like Joel."

"He's more pathetic than drugged out, but he still lives with his parents. And he plays music instead of getting a job."

"Hey, I live with my parents." He smiled, but his brows pulled together a little.

"I made an exception for you."

"I'm looking for a place."

She dropped her fork on her place. "Do you live in their basement? You're recovering from a terrible car accident. You get a pass."

"For how long?"

She shrugged. "That's up to you and your doctors, I guess."

"No, I mean, at what point would it be pathetic for me not to have a job and be living at my parents? Because I'm pretty sure I'm passed it, to be honest." He leaned back in his chair, the fun mood quickly slipping away.

She swallowed hard. Had she done that? Pissed him off by saying the wrong thing? "You're not—"

He stood up without looking at her and started packing up the food. "You done?"

She stood too. "Not even close. What's going on?"

"Nothing." He kept tidying, and because she was done with *eating*, she didn't stop him. And maybe she was done with the conversation as well.

"Fine. What time is the reception tonight?"

"Seven."

"I need to go buy golf clothes to wear tomorrow. I'll see you then." Yeah. She was done with the conversation. She had no time for that kind of whining. She grabbed her purse from her room then left the *casita* without another glance at Chase.

— —

Waiting for a date who might not be speaking to him was awkward. The old Chase wouldn't have any time for a woman who pulled the silent treatment, but when Mari did it, he found himself just wanting to make it better. Except that would require the intimacy of actually dating, or the ability to talk about feelings, and since neither advantage was on his side, he was simply screwed.

She'd come back to the suite mid-afternoon, but went straight to her room and closed the door behind her. A while later he heard her running a bath, then she turned on music. Now he waited.

At five minutes to seven, her door swung open and his heart stopped.

Mari was gorgeous, all of the time. Dark hair, flashing eyes, curvy boobs and a sweet ass.

*This* Mari was a knockout. He realized it was probably the first time he'd seen her in heels, and the extra height drew his attention to her legs. They curved in all the right places and led straight to the hem of the almost too-short little black dress she wore like a second skin. The skirt floated around her hips, but it was snug up her torso and presented her breasts as a feast that put all room service deliveries to shame. Nestled just above her cleavage was a delicate silver pendant that sparkled in the light, framed by her hair. She wore it down, which he was grateful for, because if she put it up, his fingers would get tangled in it when he—

"Do I look okay?"

He finally dragged his attention to her perfectly made up face. "Uhhhh," he started, then cleared his throat. "Yeah. That's an understatement."

She stepped closer. "You put on a different suit. Two in one day, that's gotta be a record."

His tie felt too tight—a common enough experience, he hated the damn things. But this was different. "I own a bunch of them." *Inane answer.* She didn't seem to care. She was closer still, and then right in front of him.

"I'm sorry about earlier," she said, her voice husky. Her lips were all shiny, and he was pretty sure she wouldn't have appreciated his mouth messing them up, but she was right there. Close enough to grab and hold on to, and if he did that, he'd need a taste.

"My bad, my issues. Don't worry about it." His voice grated out of him and he stuffed his hands in his pockets to keep them off her hips.

"I'll be on my best behaviour tonight," she whispered. In heels, she was still shorter than him, but kissing wouldn't be quite the deliberate act their height difference normally made it. Maybe they could accidentally make out for a bit.

"Sure." He should move back. Offer her his arm and head to the reception. Do anything other than just stand there and stare at her lips.

Even as they came closer, he didn't realize what she was doing until she let out a little sigh and pressed her hands to his shoulders, her breasts to his chest, and her mouth to his. Time froze as she held the kiss there, a simple press of skin on skin that lit a fuse inside him. A long enough fuse that she didn't realize he was affected until she pulled away, but she didn't get far before he snagged her around the waist and banded her against him with his arms.

"Not so fast, sweetheart," he muttered.

"Just getting in the role," she whispered, eyes wide.

"That's an excellent plan." He lowered his mouth to hers, and there was nothing chaste about how *he* kissed *her*. He stole her breath, then put it to good use, trailing hot, wet kisses down her neck. He pressed one last kiss to the pulse point at the dip in her collarbone, then pulled her hips tight against his. "I warned you that you get me hard when you kiss me."

Her chest rose and fell between them. She licked her still glossy lips—the magic of modern day cosmetics—and stared at him, all wild-eyed and obviously horny. Good, that made two of them. "I was just saying sorry."

"We should fight more often. I like it." He eased back. "Shall we go?"

— —

The whole way to the bar where the private reception was being held, Chase's hand was planted firmly in the small of her back. Low enough that with every step, his pinky finger must be feeling her ass jiggle. Inside, she was alternating between doing a pervy happy dance at the smoking hot kiss he'd laid on her, and quaking in fear at the thought of what might happen when they got back to the room. Well, that also made her do a happy dance. But it was more the awkward morning after that she feared. And then the flight home. And the eventual collapse of civilization as they knew it in Wardham when it all went to shit.

Which it would.

Hence the fear.

But someone needed to tell that to her private parts, because her sex was pulsing at the thought of getting naked with Chase and her breasts ached for his hands and his mouth like nothing else mattered.

*Like you didn't know what would happen when you put on heels and a little black dress.*

Hoping and *knowing* weren't the same thing.

After their grumping at lunch, she'd done some soul searching while trying on conservative shorts and polo shirts in the gift shop. She didn't need to understand Chase. He didn't owe her any answers. She was doing him a favour, in exchange for him helping her out. Okay, so the two weren't exactly equally weighted, but it wasn't like it was a hardship coming to Arizona. Being able to climb Pinnacle Peak at dawn pretty much made them even Steven.

And it occurred to her that maybe the grumping would go away if they stopped fighting the chemistry quite so hard. From the way he was holding on to her, Chase obviously agreed.

As they stepped into the bar, though, his hand fell away from her hip. One glance at his face told her something was seriously wrong. She looked ahead, and through the crowd of well-dressed, obviously wealthy people stepped a beautiful blonde woman. She wore a bright blue dress and a dazzling smile, and her gaze was pinned on Chase.

"You made it," the other woman exclaimed, throwing herself against Chase. Mari stepped aside to avoid being hit by a flailing arm, either Chase's or the blonde's, and tried not to look like a country bumpkin who didn't know what was going on.

Chase slid his hands to the blonde's waist and carefully disentangled himself. "We did, yes."

"Who's your friend?" The blonde glued herself to Chase's side and turned toward Mari. "Hi. I'm Kelly. Chase's girlfriend."

# CHAPTER NINE

"Ex-girlfriend," Chase muttered, shoving Kelly off his hip as delicately as he could manage. She was like a fucking lamprey eel.

"Potato potahto, honey." Kelly held out her hand, which Mari just stared at. "I didn't catch your name?"

Chase reached for Mari's hand, but she was too far away. When did that happen? One minute she was right where she should be, the next Kelly was in his face and all hell broke loose in his head. "Mari," he said, hoping she heard the apology in his voice. She hesitated, but slid her hand into his. "This is Mari. My current girlfriend."

"You didn't mention anyone," Kelly simpered. "Must be new."

"What are you doing here, Kel?" He ignored her pathetic suggestion that they were still talking and hoped Mari knew that they weren't.

"My new company is one of the silver-level sponsors of the tournament."

Damn. So getting her quietly removed wasn't an option. "Great," he said, not meaning it at all.

"I was hoping we could get a chance to talk."

"Sorry, we're swamped. But it was nice seeing you again."

He sidestepped his ex, wondering what he ever saw in her, and guided Mari to the relative safety of a bar table where Tommy and his wife were holding court. He made the introductions, then snagged two drinks for them off a passing tray.

"That was awkward," Tommy said with a chuckle, proving Chase's fear that this company wasn't that safe either.

"Whatever."

"You sound like a teenage girl, man." Tommy said.

Mari laughed, to herself first, then a little louder. He slid her a quick glance, relieved she wasn't still frozen in silence. "Yeah?"

"One in particular…well, she's not a teenager anymore, but boy did that sound like Audrey." She glanced around the table. "His sister," she said in explanation.

"So you guys know each other from back home?" Tommy's wife, Cara, asked, and the conversation turned neatly to Wardham, and siblings, and what they all did on their summer break. But Chase was only partially tuned in. Most of his concentration was squarely on Mari, and the walls she'd shot up between them. She stayed at his side, but she'd lost her gentle sway. She wasn't relaxed, and she sure as hell wasn't turned on anymore. *Shit.*

"Do you want to get out of here?" he whispered, getting as close to her as he dared. She tipped her head to the side, acknowledging his question but not answering right away.

"No," she finally said, turning to face him. Her eyes were unreadable, but at least she was looking at him. "Who else should you talk to?"

"Some of the coaches. The other alumni. Donors. I'll do a loop in a few minutes—you want to come with me?"

"Up to you." She pressed her lips together into a polite smile.

He touched her chin with his index finger, then slid his hand along her jaw until the silky strands of her hair tangled with his finger tips. "I want you plastered to my side all night, if you're willing."

She lifted her chin proudly and her smile got a bit bigger. "Then that's where I'll be."

"Hey, you two, get a room!"

Mari twisted away from him and winked at Tommy.

"How's the suite, by the way?"

"Great, thanks for that, man."

"No problem. The kids wouldn't have used the second room anyway, they think it's fun to pile in with us. And tonight they're at home anyway."

Mari gave them both a confused look, which Cara correctly interpreted in that freaky girl way. She leaned across the table and lowered her voice. "Getting a room is almost the same cost as hiring a driver for the night, and this way we get to participate in the whole weekend. It's a team spirit thing. Don't think about how much it costs."

"It's hard not to," Mari muttered under her breath, but when Cara told her about the public schools they sent their kids to and the chicken farm Cara grew up on, Mari started to relax.

They didn't see Kelly again until the party was winding down. She came in from the patio as they headed for the exit, but instead of trying to talk to him again, she just waved. "See you guys tomorrow," she called.

In some ways, that was worse. The sceptre of doubt hung over them as they walked back to their *casita*, and he couldn't ignore it, not if he wanted to get Mari back to the sweet, sexy, pliable woman who kissed him before the night began.

"There's nothing left between Kelly and me," he said as they walked.

"I know," she said simply, staring straight ahead.

"Thank you for coming with me tonight."

"No problem. That's why I'm here."

He clenched his jaw. Yes, but also no. "I didn't ask you to come to Arizona to run interference with my ex."

"No?" Damn, he didn't like the questioning upturn in her voice.

He slid one hand to her waist and spun her to face him. Their *casita* was just a few yards ahead, but this needed to be said right here, right now. "I wanted you here, with me, for me. No one else." Her lips parted, trembling, and her eyes were wide. He rubbed his thumb along her cheek, to the corner of her still shiny mouth. "Why did you kiss me earlier?"

— —

Her heart was beating a mile a minute in her chest, and Chase's hand on her face was driving her to distraction. She couldn't think, could barely breath, and after two hours of holding herself together, she was pretty sure she was about to burst into tears. She took a ragged breath and closed her eyes.

"Shhh," he whispered, and she gasped as he kissed her forehead. "Don't cry."

"I'm not going to cry."

"Good."

They stood there for a few minutes, and slowly but surely Mari felt herself calming down. She sighed and leaned into Chase, glad to be alone with him and wrapped in his comforting scent.

"Can I ask you again?" he rumbled, his breath brushing against her cheek.

She smiled. "Can I ask you not to?"

"Sorry, sweetheart. No hiding right now. Why'd you kiss me earlier?"

"That's what we do, right? Kiss each other to keep the world at bay?"

He pressed closer. "Does that feel like I give a fuck about the world right now?"

"Oh," she whispered, all that lost heat from earlier flooding back into her pelvis. She ached to rub against him, to share some of the flames licking inside her. If she was going to burn, she wanted company.

"That's not why you kissed me earlier, is it?"

"No." She pressed her lips together, but he leaned back enough to grab her gaze, and then he brought his thumb to her mouth again. This time he didn't stop at the corner, instead tracing all the way around the lower lip, then lowering his mouth to suck that same flesh into his mouth.

This wasn't a kiss for anyone else, or for any reason. Not an apology, nor a cover-up or an excuse. This was kissing for kissing's sake. Mouths touching, tongues tasting. Hot air and wet lips, and between them proof that when they kissed, she really did make him hard, every time.

Well, that was fair, because he made her panties damp and her thighs ache.

"We can't do this," she whispered against his mouth.

He groaned and tipped his head back. Even as she was preparing herself to pull away, she couldn't help but press her lips to the exposed skin there. Five o'clock shadow couldn't disguise the hot, salty skin she was pretty sure she was already addicted to.

"Not out here," she panted. "Inside."

He spun her around and squeezed her hips, urging her toward their room.

At the door, she twisted and pressed her back against the wood. "Wait."

"No, wrong answer."

"We're not getting naked."

"Really the wrong answer."

"I want to make out with you."

"Now we're getting warmer."

"But that's it."

He rested his arms on the door on either side of her head. His face hovered right in front of hers, his half-lidded eyes clearly communicating what he thought of her boundaries. But probably in the interest of clarity, he took a deep breath then repeated what she'd said. "That's it."

"Yeah."

He stared at her for a bit, then pressed a hard, hot kiss to her lips. "Fine, I can work with that. For now."

He reached past her and opened the door. He kissed her gently in the entrance, then harder as they got to the couch. Then he squeezed her hips again, harder this time, and settled himself in the middle seat. He patted his lap. "Come here."

His erection strained at the front of his dress pants, and she gingerly settled herself on his left thigh.

"Uh-uh, closer," he muttered, spreading his legs a bit as he arranged her legs across his body. His bare hand on her bare legs had her questioning her limits already, but despite all their flirting, they couldn't go from zero to sixty in a single night, not without talking about where they stood. And she knew Chase well enough to know that he didn't know where they stood. Trying to talk about that now would be an exercise in frustration.

And the honest truth was that she didn't know either.

But they both wanted to touch, and taste, and they could do that with their clothes on.

"So this is okay," Chase said, his voice rough and low. He ran his hand lightly down her calf.

"Yeah," she breathed, and his cock flexed against her ass. *Oh God.*

"And this…" He trailed his fingers up the inside of her knee, stopping in the middle of the exposed part of her thigh. "But not…" he slid his fingers even higher and tapped at the hem of her dress, already obscenely high on her legs. "Past this point."

"Not tonight." Even though she wanted it so badly it hurt, they needed to wait. And there was something decadent in grown-ups playing at the fooling around game. They could luxuriate in the kissing in a way she hadn't since grade eleven and the discovery of how good it felt to be filled—yeah, that was not a good place for her thoughts to go. "Not tonight," she repeated, more confidently this time, and covered his hand with hers.

"Is this a dating rule of yours," he asked as he nuzzled her neck. His stubble scratched her skin, rubbing a reminder of their intimacy into her skin that she wouldn't soon forget.

She twisted in his lap and stroked both of her hands over his jaw and into his hair. She loved the way his curls looped around her fingers, surrounding her skin with part of his being. She held his face and gave him a mock-stern look. "Are we dating?"

"No, but..." he trailed off and gave her his best sheepish, *aw shucks, I'm so cute and famous* look. He probably didn't even know he was doing it. Or maybe he did. When was the last time someone had told him no? "That's the wrong answer, isn't it?"

She shook her head and leaned in, rubbing her nose against his before she gently bit his lower lip and growled. "Honesty is never the wrong answer, Chase." She narrowed her eyes. "What's your real name?"

"You don't think it's Chase?"

"Karen, Chase, Davis and Audrey? Yeah, I guess it could be. I assumed it was a hockey nickname."

"It is. I was Chad for the first nine years of my life, and still am according to my driver's license."

"Okay. Chad, I don't think we're dating. We both agreed at the start of this that we're not in that place right now. Neither of us is looking for the complications of a relationship. And for the record, I don't have dating rules. But I think I have friends with benefits rules."

"You think?" He lifted her hips and settled her in a slightly different spot on his lap. A more *erect* spot. She wanted to point out that dry humping was *not* the same thing as kissing, but he felt far too good between her legs to justify a complaint. She held herself back from rocking—just barely—as he traced the neckline of her dress. "How many friends with benefits arrangements have you stumbled through without rules?"

"None." The admission felt more intimate than she intended, so she pushed it away with a flippant comeback. "You'll have to be the experienced one here."

Heat flared in his eyes. "Oh sweetheart, I'm plenty experienced, I assure you, but not with this."

"I find that hard to believe," she gasped as he rolled his hips beneath her. "Stop that. Tell me more about how you haven't had a lot of casual hook-ups."

His grip tightened on her hips, then he raked his hands up her sides and pulled her down toward him slowly, his gaze getting more serious with each inch. "I didn't say that. I said I don't have any experience with *this*." He took her mouth before she could protest, and this time it was a needy, hungry clash of teeth and tongues and lips. Nothing sensual or practiced. She gave right back as good as she got, pissed off that he was kissing her in the same breath as he admitted to having a history. But even though their scrolls of names probably weren't comparable, neither of them was coming to this pure as the driven snow.

And it shouldn't matter.

*But it does*, a small voice in her heart said. *It matters what kind of man he is.*

"What are your friends with benefits rule proposals?" he said when he broke away from their kiss. Both of them were breathing hard.

"First…no other *friends* while we do this." After seeing Kelly plaster herself all over Chase tonight, Mari knew she couldn't handle sharing him.

"I'm a one-woman guy," he said quietly, his gaze never leaving hers.

"Second…no rushing. We only move on to the dirty stuff when we're sure we can do it without any repercussions."

"I think you're underestimating how dirty I can make kissing on the couch, but okay. No sex this weekend."

"Really?" She didn't bother to keep the shock out of her voice. Honesty was a good thing, hadn't she just finished telling him that?

"Yes." He gave her a confused look. "What kind of assholes have you been with in the past?"

She sighed and shook her head. "The usual kind. Young, selfish, stupid." He pulled his lips together like he was holding back awful thoughts about her exes, and she pressed her fingertips to his mouth. "Never mind that."

"I mind," he said slowly, his soft, hot gaze tearing open her heart. "We do this at your pace."

She leaned in and kissed his jaw, and he twisted his face to kiss her mouth. This time it was slower than slow, his tongue sliding across hers like a striptease under a strobe light, proving that he could absolutely make kissing on the couch 100% dirty.

His hands managed to be everywhere and still stay within the safe zone at the same time. At some point, Mari ended up on her back, Chase hovering over her kissing her neck and her cleavage and then her mouth again, and it was at that point she decided that kissing was pretty much the most awesome thing ever.

So when he pulled away and she knew it wasn't just for air, she almost pouted at the loss.

"Come on, sweetheart, time for me to walk you to your door and kiss you goodnight."

Just because it was her limit didn't make climbing off the couch any easier. She took his extended hand and pulled herself up, only to find herself hauled against his very hard and deliciously broad chest once more. "Thank you," she whispered into his shirt. She'd kicked off her shoes while he was driving her out her mind with his talented tongue, and now she felt smaller than ever compared to him.

He chuckled and turned her toward her room. "You've got an odd sense of who should be grateful here, Mari. I promise you it's not the beautiful woman poured into the little black dress."

"Okay. Then...you're welcome." She blinked up at him through her eyelashes, this time putting a deliberate tease on her usual snark. This was a curious feeling, having all the options. It felt...safe.

"Come here," he muttered, cupping her neck and pulling her close again. He kissed her for the hundredth time, and she wondered at how each one felt a little different.

"Wow," she whispered when he finally let her up for air.

"Good night, Mari."

She hummed and pressed her fingers to her lips, then slowly reached across the small gap between their faces and pressed those same fingers to his mouth. "You're not such a bad guy, Chad."

He lifted his brow in surprise. "From last names to formal first name, eh?" He nipped at her fingertips. "I guess you can call me whatever you want."

He pressed one last quick kiss to her mouth, then stepped back. One step, then more. She stayed in the doorway to her room until he reached his, and then she dashed inside and threw herself on the bed.

# CHAPTER TEN

"You look like you need coffee." Chase had been up long enough to order coffee and bagels and stretch out his leg. A round of golf should be fine, but the last thing he wanted was for his limp to become more pronounced over the course of the day.

He rounded the table and pulled Mari close. Her hair was standing up on end and she was still all sleep-warm and rumpled in a tank top and shorts. He'd much rather spend the day in bed with her than head out on the golf course.

"Someone did a good job of turning me on last night," Mari muttered under her breath. "I had a lot of distracting dreams."

"I slept like a baby." He laughed as she growled and shook her face against his chest. "You should have taken care of yourself." He had, and he'd gone off like a rocket ship.

She mumbled something quietly.

"Pardon?"

She twisted away and poured herself a cup of coffee, then took a sip. "I did," she admitted with a sideways glance in his direction. "Twice."

*Jesus.* That was a gorgeous picture. "Will you tell me about it?"

She shook her head with a smile.

"How about you show me sometime?"

This time she hesitated before shrugging. "Yeah, maybe. If you're doing it at the same time."

He moved behind her, going slow enough that he

wouldn't jostle her coffee. He wrapped his arms around her waist and curved his torso around hers. "That is a devilish thing to say, Beadie."

She grinned down at her cup. "I know."

"I like it." He nipped at her ear. "Can we make a date for that when we get back to Wardham?"

"Make a date?" She twisted and lifted one eyebrow at him. She was smirking. "That sounds perilously close to not faking things." Yeah, it did. He didn't know what to do about that. "Let's just see how things go. Maybe we won't even be speaking by the end of this trip."

"Just how awful do you think today is going to go?"

She widened her eyes in mock horror. "Oh my god, so awful."

"Shut up." He kissed her neck and lightly smacked her hip. "Hurry up and eat, we've got to be at the golf course in an hour."

The day ended up being the opposite of awful. They were put in a foursome with a local businessman and his wife, who wasn't a big golfer either, so Mari had someone to commiserate with.

Even though she'd never golfed before, she'd been a pretty willing pupil. And Chase had quite enjoyed wrapping himself around her as he demonstrated proper swing technique.

The hunt for an errant ball in a stand of trees that ended up with making out against a tree hadn't been bad, either.

By the time the barbecue dinner was wrapping up, Chase was ready to head back to their suite. He'd lost sight of Mari, who'd been dragged off by the woman they'd spent the day with—who apparently took the mantra that girls went to the bathroom in groups quite seriously—but in anticipation of their imminent departure he'd stepped to the bar and called ahead to the resort, arranging for a bottle of champagne and a fruit and chocolate tray to be delivered ahead of them. Might as well milk the last few hours of room service availability for all it was worth.

"You've been hiding from me," a voice purred behind him and Chase stiffened.

"Kelly," he sighed as he turned around. "Not hiding. We just don't have anything else to talk about. I met with my lawyer the other day, you'll get a letter from him next week about the condo." They were giving her a generous offer—she could buy him out now at a reduced amount, or wait until she sold if she'd prefer not to take a mortgage again. He wasn't interested in screwing her over, but he was done owning property with her.

She stepped closer and pressed her hand against his chest, a pouting frown on her face. "I wish you'd asked me to go with you. We had a life together and—"

He grabbed her wrist and lifted her hand, firmly enough that she wouldn't mistake it for anything other than a *get your stinkin' mitt off my body* action, and cut her off before she could go any further. "We dated. I moved in with you because it was *convenient*. That was a mistake. We didn't have a life together, not really. And even if you hadn't cheated on me with that douchebag, we never would have lasted. I don't know what you're looking for, Kelly, but I'm not that guy."

Over Kelly's shoulder he caught sight of Mari. She walked toward them in a purposefully unhurried way, and he couldn't read the look on her face. How much had she heard?

"You ready to go?" she asked. Her voice was as neutral as her face, but there was an uncomfortable stiffness to the question.

"Yep. Totally done here."

"He's just going to break your heart," Kelly said from behind him. Chase willed himself not to react. It didn't matter what she said.

Mari stepped closer and slid her arm around his waist. "Don't worry, hon. My heart isn't what I'm letting him play with."

They walked arm-in-arm to the valet stand but it felt like a performance, and sure enough, Mari crossed her arms as soon as they were alone in the car.

"Sorry about that," he offered lamely.

"What? Oh. Yeah, you really know how to pick them."

"Does it make a difference that Kelly's the first difficult ex I've had?"

"How many easy exes have you had?" He saw that for the rhetorical question it was and didn't bother to answer. She looked out the window, then down at her hands. It took almost the whole drive back to their *casita* for her to speak again. "Last night when I said you weren't such a bad guy?"

"You might have spoken too soon?" He shrugged. "I probably have some growth to do in that area."

She laughed. "No. I meant it. But I'd forgotten that you've got some…baggage. Is this a smart idea?"

He got out of the car and went around to her side. She waited for him to open her door, but then gave him an exaggerated eye-roll as she got out.

"Is what a smart idea?"

"Us. Kissing. Maybe more." She ducked under the arm he'd left against the car door.

He locked up and followed her, catching up just as she opened the door to their suite. She stopped as soon as she saw the candles, wine and fruit set up. Frankly, he was impressed they'd come and gone so quickly himself.

He gave her a wide berth, but he didn't avoid her question. "I don't want to make any false promises. Like you say, I've got baggage. But you make me happy, Mari." He shoved his hands in his pockets to keep from closing the gap between them and grabbing hold of her.

She stood there staring at the romantic set-up and he cursed himself for the idea. It assumed more than he was allowed and blurred the lines in an unhelpful way. And it wasn't really either of them.

"Honesty's the best policy, right?"

She glanced back at him over her shoulder. "Yes."

"Then yeah. I think this is smart. Because you've seen me warts and all. You know I've got baggage. And we're not pretending."

She spun in a slow circle, a pensive look on her face. "I could see how someone would be reluctant to give you up, if this is how you date someone."

"I was just thinking that the champagne wasn't really a smart move."

She rolled her eyes. "I might be a cynic, but champagne is *always* a good move."

"So are we okay?"

She slowly nodded. "Yeah. We're okay. I'm going to get my suit on. Want to meet me in the pool in five minutes?"

In his pockets, his hands slowly unclenched. He hadn't realized he'd fisted them that tightly until the circulation started to return. He grinned. "That sounds perfect."

She smiled, a coy little play of something mysterious across her face, and as she reached her room, she spun around. "Chase?"

*Invite me in*, he thought spontaneously. *Let's put all this noise aside and just get naked.* He knew it was wishful thinking, but damn, getting lost in Mari sounded like a bang-up way to salvage what was left of the day. "Yeah?" he asked.

"Bring the champagne."

Okay. That wasn't the same as sex, but it was pretty damn good. "You got it."

— —

Mari floated on her back. The sun had just set and they'd each had two glasses of champagne. "I'm getting cold," she said to the dark sky.

From a few feet away, Chase laughed. She liked the sound of it, rough and amused. His laugh wrapped around her toes and worked its way up her legs, and she yanked herself upright before it could reach anywhere dangerous. He was watching her in that lazy, half-lidded way of his, and all of a sudden there wasn't enough air in the entire state of Arizona to fill her lungs.

"Come here," he said, and she did because maybe if he held her, she'd be able to breathe again. "This hasn't been the greatest trip for you," he said as he settled her on his lap. "What do you want to do tomorrow before we leave?"

"Outlet shopping," she blurted out, then blushed. Would he think that was cheesy?

"You got it. My mom's favourite is in Anthem. We'll go there first, and if there's time, we can go to Arizona Mills after. It's close to the airport."

She blinked at him. *Huh.*

"What?"

"I don't know," she whispered. "I think the wine is going to my head."

"I have two sisters, a clothes-horse for a brother, and a mother who spent most of the last five years living in an RV, traveling around the States. Is it such a surprise I know about the shopping in the city I lived for nine years?"

She shrugged. "It's strangely helpful information."

"I like to surprise you."

He'd certainly done that many times over on this trip.

"Hot tub time." She blinked at him again and he laughed. "Yeah, you're tipsy. And cold, remember?"

He slid her off his lap, then climbed out before offering her his hand. When she joined him on the deck, he wrapped his arms around her and covered her mouth with his. She opened readily, hungry for more. She teased her tongue against his, enjoying the way his grip tightened. "Not so cold now," she said when he broke away.

"Hot tub, you minx."

She swayed her hips deliberately as she walked to the corner of the pool to grab the bottle of champagne. "Not without our friend here."

"I think you've had enough."

"And I think we're on vacation, sort of, and I'm a bartender who never gets to cut loose. Well, rarely. I mean, there are the occasional girls' nights."

"I've heard of those. Gossip and giggles."

She swung around and pointed the almost empty bottle at him. "I'm not a gossip."

"No." He grinned, a slow, sexy smile that made her want to get in the hot tub *naked*. "That you aren't. Mari Beadie is a vault. One of the many things I like about you."

Now they were talking. "Mmmm. Tell me some of the other things."

He pointed to the tub. "In."

She shrugged. *Okay*. That was like twisting her rubber arm. The warm, bubbly water made her hum as she sank onto the first level of underwater seats.

"I like the noises you make, for one." He slid in next to her, his thigh pressing against hers, and she turned her face to look at him. Steam rose around him—around the two of them—and it felt like they were all alone in the world.

"Kiss me," she whispered.

He leaned in. "I like how much you like kissing," he muttered before nipping at her bottom lip. She didn't usually, but there was something about sharing such an intimate act with Chase—it wasn't weird or invasive, he knew just how much tongue to use and when, and he always left her wanting more.

A lot more.

"I like your boundaries," he said, although the rough edge to his voice said at least part of him had trouble with them. "They're smart. *You're* smart."

She shook her head. "More kisses."

He gave her one, but it was brief. "I think it's bedtime." She wiggled in his lap, and for a moment he held her hips firmly in place as he let out a slow, controlled breath. She liked that little indication that he was shaken by their connection—and that he was fighting it. She sure as hell was. "Fine, we can stay here for a bit."

She slid off his lap again and curled up beside him, tipping her face to the sky. "Different stars here."

"Yeah."

"Do you miss Arizona?"

"Nah. It was a good run while I was here, but Wardham is my home." She thought about what he'd said on their drive about leaving as a teenager. He'd had his fair share of testing the truth of that statement, for sure. "How about you? Ever get the urge to head to a city for a while?"

She nodded, then shook her head, then groaned.

"Damn. That sounds like a good story."

"I don't know. I like travelling. It's almost like I think I *should* want to leave, because it's not cool to just live in the same place forever. And I could get a job anywhere…" She drifted off. She was rambling. It didn't matter.

Chase glided his hand over her knee, but instead of pressing higher, he went the other direction. He squeezed her calf, lifting her foot into his lap. "Lean back," he said quietly. She closed her eyes and tipped her head against the side of the tub. "Tell me more about what's got you so conflicted."

"Why?"

"We have to do something to keep me from trying to get you naked," he said wryly.

"It wouldn't be hard," she admitted.

"I know. Hence the question. And no more kisses for a bit."

"Boo. I like how you kiss."

"Noted. Now talk."

So she did. She spilled her guts about the one-in-a-million shot at recording contracts and her fears about never earning more than minimum wage as a performer. She talked about her brothers and the weird dynamic with her oldest brother, Sam, and her parents.

When she trailed off, he waited a couple of minutes before talking again.

"I'd forgotten that your birth father left."

She made a face. She'd never met the man. He'd left her mother when she found out she was pregnant with twins—with two boisterous boys already bouncing around their farmhouse. Her real dad, Mark Beadie, was the man who'd married a single mother of four children and given the whole lot his name, formally adopting four children under the age of seven as soon as the legal hoops could be leapt through.

"Sam's a year younger than me, right?"

"He's thirty-one."

"Two years, then. It's a shame he's not closer to your dad."

"And yet they insist on working together. Fighting together, really."

"I get that. I'll probably never give up on trying to live up to my dad's expectations." He said it so casually, so matter-of-factly that she'd have fallen over if she wasn't floating in water.

"What?"

He looked at her with genuine confusion on his face. "What what?"

"Of course your dad is proud of you." He'd been in the NHL. It was pretty much the Canadian dream for all fathers of their sons.

"Nah." He made a face. "I mean, he's been proud in the past, but that's all kind of slid away."

"You've moved on to the next stage of your life, that's all. It doesn't undo your past successes."

"It doesn't matter now." But his voice said otherwise, and even through her tipsy haze she could hear the bite of pain.

"You know what?"

He cocked his head to the side and smiled. "What?"

"If your dad knew just how good a kisser you are, he'd be really proud of you." She barely got a shriek out before she slid under water, because he yanked her forward off her seat by the leg he'd been rubbing so nicely just a few seconds earlier. When she came up for air, she was in his arms and straddling him once again. "We have to stop meeting like this," she whispered, water running down her cheeks from her sopping wet hair.

"I don't know what I did to deserve your sassy mouth, woman, but I like it. Now shut up."

He kissed her thoroughly then, in the hot tub, then wrapped her in a towel and kissed her good night half a dozen times on the way to her bedroom door.

# CHAPTER ELEVEN

After packing up, they met a few people in the restaurant for brunch, then went shopping before heading to the airport.

Chase enjoyed himself more than he thought he would. And Mari spent just as much time choosing things for him as she did herself.

"Why don't you get that?" he asked when she took a long, regretful look at a silky midnight blue dress before putting it back on the rack.

She shrugged. "I can't get carried away by the fairy tale fun of this trip. I can't afford it. I've already bought way too much."

He looked at the two bags she was carrying. Jesus, her definition of extravagance needed some work. "I'll get it for you."

"Oh, no." She motored away from the dress rack. He snagged the dress and followed.

"Come on. Maybe there will be another event where I need you on my arm. Only fair for me to cover any related expenses."

She stopped in her tracks and turned around slowly. "Like an escort?" A thick lock of hair tumbled over her forehead and she brushed it out of the way. She didn't looked pissed, just amused, but he knew better than to play with fire.

"Like a friend doing a favour—and besides, your legs looked great in it. Really, you'd be doing *me* the favour by letting me see you wear it."

"That's ridiculous," she murmured, but she let him pull

her close and kiss her softly.

"This weekend has been fairy tale fun?" he asked as he rubbed his nose against her cheek and down along her jaw.

Her cheek warmed against his. "Yes." She smoothed her hands against his chest and pushed them apart. Her eyes flashed dark for a minute before she ducked her head. "But back to real life tomorrow."

"We could run away together if you'd rather." Her hair fell around her face, but he just make out that she was biting her lip. "What is it?"

"Nah, nothing." She lifted her face and shook her head, eyes bright. "Come on, you can buy me earrings off the clearance rack to match."

"Wow, don't go crazy now."

But it hadn't been nothing, because she managed to dodge his next attempt to kiss her, and by the time their plane touched down in Detroit that night, she'd erected some painfully platonic walls between them.

It was late, and she needed to work the next day. And he wasn't an idiot. Something significant had changed between them while they were away, but neither of them wanted to get too involved. He knew people who'd done the casual, long-term thing. It was possible. But maybe it didn't seem so feasible to Mari.

They'd find some time to talk—soon.

When he pulled up in front of her apartment, she put her hand firmly on his arm when he went to get out.

"Thank you for this weekend," she said, then cleared her throat. "I really did have a wonderful time."

"Am I sensing a but there?" He was a big boy. He wasn't used to being dumped, but he could handle it.

She leaned across the cab of the truck and pressed a gentle kiss to his cheek. "No." She sighed.

"Okay, I didn't imagine that."

"Good night, Chase."

He twisted toward her and cupped her neck. "You made this weekend wonderful." He pressed his mouth against hers, tasting her lips just for a minute before easing back. "And for the record, *that's* how we kiss goodnight. Until you tell me we're done."

— —

Chase was damn addictive. Mari needed to get out of his truck before she crawled into his lap and threw all caution to the wind.

And maybe she would, but not tonight. Heart thumping, lips tingling, she did an ungainly wiggle backwards until she hit the door, then she turned and found the handle. She heard an amused chuckle behind her, but she didn't look back.

It wouldn't help anything to know that Chase found her cute when flustered.

She managed to avoid him for the next few days. He stayed away on Monday. Came in to the bar for lunch on Tuesday, but they were thankfully jammed and while he watched her—deliciously confident as he drank his beer, like he knew that his gaze made her burn up on the inside, no matter how cool she pretended to be on the outside. She didn't work on Wednesday, and she turned her phone off and locked the downstairs door, so even if he did come looking for her, she wouldn't know.

It meant absolutely nothing that she looked out her windows at least a dozen times that day, searching for a black pick-up truck.

Her luck ran out on Thursday afternoon. He came in later than usual, and instead of sunscreen he smelled faintly of chlorine. It was ridiculously sexy. She needed to have her head examined. But maybe because he was yummy, and definitely because he'd given her space, she couldn't help herself from starting a conversation.

"Is the lake getting too cold for a swim?" she asked after he ordered some lunch.

He grinned. "Look at you, being all detective-y. Yeah, I

went into the city to swim at the university. Parking was a nightmare. I've decided to get myself on the community centre planning committee. We need a better pool here."

She rolled her eyes. Ridiculously sexy and out-of-touch with reality. "Sure. Like anyone else in Wardham needs a competition-length pool."

"Build it and they will come."

She paused. Actually, that was a good idea—and if Chase could attract any corporate sponsorship to the project, it might pay for itself. "You should talk to Carrie Nixon about it."

He waved his hand. "I was kind of kidding."

"No, this is a great idea!" She clapped her hands together, then reached across the bar and tapped his forearm in excitement. "I'll go get your sandwich." And she skipped back to the kitchen. Chase didn't *need* something to do, but getting involved with the community centre would be good for him.

*And then what?* And then nothing. She didn't have a long-term stake in Chase being happy. She just wanted him to find something to care about. *He seems interested in caring about you.* Nope, that wasn't an option. They were friends. The chemistry between them would eventually fade and it would be best if they didn't have any complicating history—like having seen each other naked.

Although *not* having seen Chase naked would always count high on her list of life-long disappointments.

It was on this depressing thought that she delivered his lunch. At least she'd have the memory of their getaway. And whatever kisses he managed to sneak past her defences before she got up the courage to officially end their fake relationship.

And like he could read her mind, Chase took the basket and set it aside. "You're avoiding me."

"I'm serving you food. We had a whole conversation about a pool. How could I—" She gasped as he slid his hand across the bar and took a firm hold on her wrist.

He looked at her expectantly.

She glanced around the near empty bar, then sighed and leaned forward onto her elbows. This wasn't a conversation she wanted to have, but she wouldn't hide from him. He deserved more than that. "I'm not *avoiding* you. I'm just…back to the regular routine."

"Are we pretending Arizona didn't happen?"

*Never.* But she needed to put their relationship back in a box she could handle. "No. The next time you need me to play your girlfriend, just shout. This weekend was fun."

"Fun." He cracked his jaw. "I thought it was a hell of a lot more than that. I thought we got close to something there."

She blinked slowly, then let out a long, slow breath. "Maybe we did. But now that we're back, it doesn't seem wise."

"Wise." He nodded slowly, but in a way that didn't suggest agreement. At all.

She thought about telling him about her upcoming trip to Toronto. To underline just how different their lives were. But he was a smooth-talker, in his own way, and he'd have an answer for everything. Sharing wouldn't get her anywhere other than flat on her back beneath him, and no matter how much her body liked that idea, her head knew it was a mistake.

"But if I need you…"

She frowned. His tone had a sharp edge she didn't like, but that was how she'd framed it.

He grimaced and tried again, his voice softer this time. "I mean, to help me out."

Even if they cooled things in secret, she could be whatever he needed in public. "Of course."

"And what if I just need Mari?"

She felt her lips part and she paused herself before asking the question that she knew would open the lid on that box she desperately wanted to shove them back into. But hell, he knew the temptation wasn't one sided. "For what?"

"For kissing. Or more. I thought we were going to take our—" He hesitated. "Our arrangement to the next level."

— — —

Her face clouded over for a second. Damnit, that hadn't been the right choice of words at all.

"Like I said in Phoenix," she said with cool detachment, pushing away from the bar. She grabbed a bar cloth and started polishing the countertop, her gaze deliberately avoiding his now. "I don't have any experience with a strictly *friends with benefits* deal, but you can't have any expectations of getting more physical."

"Hey, I was going to say relationship, but I thought that might scare you. You know I'm not that kind of guy."

She nodded and glanced to the door like she wanted a flood of customers to come in and save her from talking to the guy whose tongue had been down her throat apparently one too many times.

Fine, he could take a hint.

But he wasn't going to storm off, and he wasn't going to make a scene. He pulled out his phone, picked up his sandwich and went back to being the old Chase. Just what she wanted. Or what she was trying to pretend she wanted.

He couldn't forget how hot she'd been in his arms. How close they'd come to getting naked—multiple times—over the weekend. He'd thought he'd been doing the right thing, going slow and stoking the fires between them.

Maybe they should've just had a weekend fling and been done with it.

"Chase?" He jerked his head up. His sandwich was long gone, and Mari tentatively pointed to his basket. "Can I take that?"

He nodded, stood, and pulled some cash out of his wallet. "I'm going fishing with my dad for the weekend," he muttered without looking up at her. "Want to have dinner some time next week?"

She didn't answer. He had two choices—assume her silence was a polite no, and walk away, or take advantage of what he knew was on his side and make her burn a little.

He hadn't survived nine years in the NHL without learning the value of sometimes playing dirty. He looked up, caught her gaze, and lowered his voice. "Tell you what. You don't need to decide now. Just keep thinking about how good it feels when you're riding my lap and you can feel exactly what you do to me."

Two hot pink circles popped onto her cheeks. "That's not fair," she whispered.

"Sorry, sweetheart. I have a feeling I wouldn't know how to play fair when it comes to hanging on to you." Her pretty little nose flared at that, and he stepped back. "Let me know what night works for you."

She pressed her lips together and took a deep breath, then smiled slowly like she knew something he didn't. Not a big stretch on the ol' imagination. "Well, the joke's on you. I'm actually out of town for most of next week."

"Why?" Like he had any right to ask. But he had, so he left it there between them.

She slowly shook her head. "That's for me to know and for you to stew on for a bit." Her eyes softened. "And when I get back, maybe we can go for a drive."

"Something tells me there's a PG-13 limit to what you'll allow me to do in a car."

She shrugged and leaned over the bar, showing him a decent amount of cleavage. "If you're good, maybe we can park and hold hands for a while."

He knew she was teasing. Fair turnaround for him playing the chemistry card. But all he could think about was how soft the tops of her breasts were and how unfair it was that he couldn't one hundred percent verify that the rest of them were equally amazing, even though he had no doubt. "Sounds like a deal," he said with a wink.

And she licked her lips.

Yeah. They had too much chemistry to be done before

they even got started.

And underneath that...they weren't just friends who'd considered adding a benefits side arrangement, they really were *friends*. And she was doing a better job than he was of protecting that friendship. And he needed to get out of her face before he did anything to damage the fragile peace offering she'd just given him.

He stuffed his hands in his pockets to keep from doing something stupid like hauling her over the bar top and kissing her senseless, and headed for the door.

So they were back into the friends that eye-fucked holding pattern. At least they were still friends. She was probably his *only* friend, which he knew wasn't ideal despite his solitary nature. Spending some time with the guys in Arizona had made that point.

And that annoying thought was still on his mind the next day when Dr. Mettner showed up for his weekly session. It was probably time for him to tell her to stop coming around. But that would mean admitting to his father that he was as fixed as he was going to be...so instead he let the good doctor into his loft and grabbed them both bottles of water.

"It's been a week since our last appointment, Chase. How have you been?" The psychologist sat on the couch, her tote bag full of notes on his neuroses at her feet.

She really was the best match for him, all things considered. She was about his age, and a serious triathlete herself, so she had a good handle on the athlete's mind. Plus she had a dry sense of humour that kept her on this side of annoying him even when she casually dug where he didn't want one digging.

"I've been fine."

"How was the trip?"

"Good." He took a deep breath. "Productive. I met with my lawyer. Wrapped things up with Kelly once and for all."

She dug this way and that, but there wasn't anything there to talk about. He glanced at his clock. Ten minutes seemed to crawl by at quarter time pace during these sessions.

"You were worried about how you'd be received."

Had he been? That had faded to the background pretty quickly. "I ended up worrying more about how Mari felt about Kelly being a bitch."

"You took Mari with you?"

Had he not told her that he'd planned to do that? Maybe not. "Yes."

"Interesting."

"What does that mean?"

She lifted her brow slightly. "It means it is of interest."

He wanted to growl at her that she didn't get to pull apart his relationship with Mari, but she hadn't said anything yet. The fierce protectiveness he was feeling might be unnecessary.

She just smiled.

"I didn't tell you that I was taking her because it's not a big deal."

She shook her head. "Or because it was just a given to you."

He frowned. "No…she didn't want to go. I must not have told you because maybe I didn't know she was coming at our last session."

"Interesting."

"What?"

"Why didn't she want to go?"

He leaned back and crossed his arms. "She's worried about complicating things between us, I guess. Listen, I don't want to talk about Mari."

"Why not?"

"Because you don't get to pick at her motivations. It doesn't matter why she was reluctant. We went. We had a great time. I'm not going to hurt her."

His shrink looked at him with bland appraisal, like he hadn't just snapped at her. "I don't think you'll hurt her."

*Mari does.* "Fine. We should talk about why I don't want to work."

"Okay. Tell me more about that."

"I need to figure out what's next in my life. Not hockey." Admitting that was easier than he thought.

"It's taken you a long time to bring that up on your own."

This was the part where he was supposed to continue talking. Still a challenge.

"Can I step back a bit in the conversation?"

"Mari's off-limits."

"Not that far back, but that's interesting, too."

He stared at her, waiting. Not giving an inch.

"Do you really want another career?"

*I want to be good enough for her.* "It seems kind of pathetic not to do something."

"People have talked to you about investments? Speaking opportunities?"

*Yes and yes.* "I'm not a people person."

"You don't say." Dr. Mettner looked down at her notes. "Which brings us back to what you're doing with your time here."

"What do you mean?"

"Maybe you don't need a job. Maybe you need a social life."

"I'm going fishing with my dad this weekend."

She pressed her lips together and waited.

He rolled his eyes. "Fine. I'll find someone to play golf with."

She laughed. "Or you could do something you're passionate about."

"I like golf."

"That's the problem, though, isn't it? You loved hockey. Golf isn't going to replace that."

"I *love* hockey. No past tense."

"Right, I'm sorry. So what do you love?"

*Dark wavy hair, lips pursed in thought...* He glanced up, feeling almost guilty, but Dr. Mettner just nodded. He frowned. "What?"

"Find more things that put that look on your face."

# CHAPTER TWELVE

This was better than golf.

Apparently all it took was a single sentence to his sisters—"I'm looking for someone who isn't big on small talk to go rock climbing with or something"—and they'd leapt on their phones.

Now he was twenty metres up a bluff face searching for a good footing. His arms burned, his fingers were turning numb, and he was happier than he'd been all week. Since Mari had disappeared on her mysterious road trip.

Ten feet to his left, Evan West popped into his peripheral vision. "Slowing down, man?"

Chase narrowed his eyes and tried to picture where that notch in the rock had been that he'd had his hands on just a minute before. *There.* He pushed himself higher, back in the lead but just barely. By the time they hauled themselves up, they were both drenched with sweat—and both ready to claim the fastest time. Evan had started first, but Chase had caught up—and passed him—but at the top...

"You're speedy as fuck for someone still recovering from an accident," Evan spit out.

Chase shrugged. "My last surgery was six months ago. I'm as good as I'm going to get."

"You're pretty good." Evan took a big glug of water. "But hockey's done?"

"Yeah. I'm old. Time to let that dream go."

Evan just snorted. He was three years older than Chase, although he didn't look it.

"You're in crazy shape for a businessman," Chase said

grudgingly.

"I'm dating a cross fit trainer right now. It has a few advantages." Evan rolled onto his side, then slowly stood and unbuckled his safety harness.

Chase did the same, then they collected the rest of their gear and walked back to their cars.

Evan held out his hand, and they exchanged a quick shake. "This was good, man. We should do it again next week."

"Deal." Chase helped Evan load the gear bags into his trunk, then he unlocked his truck and checked his messages. Nothing from Mari. She was due back today, he was pretty sure. Audrey had said something like that when he got back from his fishing weekend with his dad—a weekend that managed to go by without any talking at all, unless one counted baseball and fishing-related chatter.

But Chase couldn't very well grill Audrey on when his supposed girlfriend would return home. So he'd just filed away that nugget and waited. Swam a lot, ran a bit, and climbed a bluff. Now he was done waiting.

He thumbed over to his text messages window and hit compose. **Miss you. On my lap and in my passenger seat. Looking forward to that drive.**

A week was too long to go without seeing her. Frankly, a day was hard.

His dick objected.

His heart objected too. It wasn't a line. He *missed* her, in the disturbingly serious kind of way.

Maybe he could find someone who liked boxing. That sounded like a good way to be social right about now.

— —

Mari had looked at Chase's text message more times than she could count since returning home late the night before. She pulled out her phone to read it again, because she was addicted to the way her tummy fluttered at the words, "*on my lap*".

She missed him. Hard.

*So tell him that, you ninny.* As it had the night before and first thing when she woke up, her thumb itched to respond. This time she'd actually tapped the text message box when the phone rang.

Saved by the Stella.

"Hello?"

"Can you hear me?" Stella whispered.

"Yes…where are you?"

"At work. Can you come to a games night at Carrie's tonight?"

*Nope. Gotta make up with my fake boyfriend, sorry.* But there was something about Stella's whispered question that had Mari biting back the negative answer. "What's going on?"

"Oh, you know. Just the usual. Social gatherings aren't my forte." Something thumped over the line and Stella swore.

"What are you doing?"

"Nothing."

"Stell, where are you?"

"I'm in a closet. Don't worry about it."

"Why—"

"Because I panicked, that's why. I heard Beth and Ty talking about tonight, and I knew I needed to secure reinforcements."

*Ah ha.* She knew it. "So you went and hid in a closet and called me? That makes sense."

"Where else should I have gone?"

"I don't know…outside?"

"This was closer."

Mari laughed, then promised to pick her friend up at seven. Chase could wait another day.

*No, he really can't,* her heart said.

As if his ears—or maybe other parts of his anatomy— were burning, her phone rang again barely ten seconds after she'd made the decision not to call him.

"Hello there." She smiled despite herself.

"You're at work."

"I am."

"I sent you a text message yesterday."

"I got it. I liked it."

"You didn't respond. I wasn't sure…"

She smiled. "I've looked at it many, many times since yesterday. I just…" She trailed off. She didn't really have an end to that sentence.

"It's okay. Are you busy? Should I come by and help you carry some beer from the back?"

She laughed. "Maybe."

"What are you doing after your shift?"

"I'm busy, unfortunately. Stella's roped me into a game night at her cousin's place."

"Ian? I know Ian. Can I invite myself along?" A horn blared in the background, both over the phone and outside the bar, and then Chase was standing in the doorway.

She hung up, her pulse doing burlesque girl-style high kicks, and waved her hand at the couple of older guys sitting at the bar. "You guys good?"

"They're good," Chase said as he stalked down the length the pub, meeting her at the gap where the bar stopped. He didn't bother with the storeroom this time, just slid his hand over her shoulder and cupped her neck, holding her in place as he kissed her.

Oh, she'd missed him hard. He tasted like cool fall air and cinnamon coffee. She wanted to climb inside his shirt and take up residence next to his beating heart.

"Hi," she whispered, her own heart thumping in her chest.

"You could have called me when you got home last night. I would have come over and done this then."

"It was late." And she'd been trying to make a point about not missing him, although that seemed silly now.

"I was up." He released her long enough to sit on one of the stools and pull her loosely between his legs. "And now you're going to a games night without me. I'm hurt."

His grin said otherwise. It said all sorts of even more dangerous things, like he was damned pleased to have her hips in his hands and he was just happy to kiss her again.

"I didn't think it was your kind of thing," she offered slowly.

He shrugged. "It's not. But maybe I need to expand my horizons."

"There's a secret awkward back story I'll need to fill you in on and you can't tell anyone."

"Seriously? Is this high school?"

"If you don't want to come—"

"Okay, fine. Secret drama. Check."

"And Carrie has a rule that all cell phones need to be turned off for the duration of the games."

"Oh, come on." He groaned and pulled her closer, burying his face in her neck. "This just gets better and better." The words rumbled through her chest and she couldn't help but laugh.

"I missed you, too," she whispered as she wrapped her arms around his neck. "You'll have a good time?"

"Or die trying."

"I told Stella I'd pick her up…" Mari trailed off. She didn't know what the rules were here.

"Okay. I'll pick you up. We'll make out a little. Then we'll swing by her farm and get her before going to have all the games night fun we can possibly handle."

— —

Ian and Carrie Nixon had a comfortable, modern bungalow out in the country, with a large family room.

Two long sofas sat across from each other, and between them on either side were oversized armchairs. *Chair and a half*, Chase vaguely recalled them being called by an interior designer on a show he'd watched with his mom early in his recovery. He'd never quite seen the point before, but with

Mari curled up against his side and a cold beer in his hand, he was starting to understand the appeal.

On the large square coffee table in the middle of the room sat *Trivial Pursuit, Settlers of Catan, Battleship, Pictionary,* and a couple of decks of cards. Something told him poker wasn't really a possibility, though. They were the decoy. *Settlers* glared at him, all cheerfully colourful, as if saying, *slap on a smile, buddy, it's Happy Night.*

He wasn't *unhappy.* Not being able to pull out his phone was kind of annoying, though.

As if the thought of their bossy hostess summoned her, Carrie swept into the room with a tray of snacks. She was a curvy, beautiful woman with bright red hair—not like Stella's, but proudly from a bottle—and flashing eyes. And the things she could do with food...it was hard to stay mad about forced socialization when she set an artichoke and Asiago dip down right within his reach.

They were just waiting for Ty West, who'd been two years ahead of Chase in school but they knew each other from around—he'd done a few local celebrity-type appearances at the winery—and Beth Stewart, who had organized his sister's wedding, and her fiancé Finn. Chase had thought Beth was single, but Mari and Stella had filled him in on their whirlwind courtship on the drive over. The things he missed when he buried his head in his phone, Mari had teased.

There was some truth to what she said.

And once everyone else arrived and they dived into *Trivial Pursuit,* playing on two teams, it turned out that games night wasn't so bad.

"Get that shit-eating grin off your face, man." Ty whipped a baguette slice at him, but Chase easily snatched it from the air and stuffed it in his mouth.

"What can I say? I know a bit of trivia."

"A bit?" Mari looked up at him from the nestled-in position she hadn't shifted from since they started playing. "That's an understatement."

Their pie had five pieces in it and they were marching like the Germans toward their sixth piece—and it was Sports & Leisure.

"What are the chances that the quiet boy genius over there doesn't know his football history?"

Chase tried to look innocent, but he couldn't. There was no chance of that. He'd been raised on sports, all of them, and not just the playing. The history, the stars, the stats. The trivia.

"The Millers might happen to own all known editions of *Trivial Pursuit*. Did I forget to mention that?"

"Mari, you brought a ringer with you," Carrie laughed. Mari just shrugged and leaned into him.

Chase looked down at her, a little surprised at just how…cuddly she was being. Now that he thought about it, she was quiet, too. "You okay?"

"Yeah, just sleepy. And thirsty. Could you get me some water?"

He disentangled himself and went to the kitchen.

Ty and Finn followed, clearly on similar beverage seeking missions.

"Games nights were invented by women who like that *we're on a team* idea," Ty groused.

Chase rolled his eyes. "No offence man, but you've got that all wrong. It's the painful prodigy of geeks who didn't understand what they were inflicting on those of us with dates."

"Right. Inflicted. Says the man almost single-handedly winning this game."

"Don't worry, I'm sure you'll kick my ass at that *Settlers* game. I don't know anything about farming." He ducked as Ty swiped a lazy hook at his arm.

Finn laughed, but then mumbled something about them both being idiots.

"What?" Ty pointed his beer bottle. "You're having a good time?"

"Beth is. And when we get home, *I* get to have a good

time with happy Beth. I'd walk on glass to keep her smiling. This is nothing."

Chase thought about Mari not caring one way or another if he'd come tonight. But since they'd arrived, she'd been glued to him. He frowned and turned back to Ty. "He makes a good point. We've got motivation that you're lacking. And it's not like anyone dragged you here. Why not just leave?"

Ty shifted uncomfortably. "Beth made it sound like fun."

"You don't get to reap the rewards of Beth thinking this is fun," Finn growled possessively, and Chase could identify with the man. He didn't want Mari cuddled up with anyone else, either. Ever.

"Come on, man. She's like a sister to me. Drop it."

"And she might be the only woman in Essex County you haven't yet turned your eye to."

"Don't worry. I know some women are off-limits. Besides, you two are made for each other, much as it pains me to say it."

Five questions later, victory was declared. Chase exchanged high-fives with Ian and Carrie, but when he turned back to Mari, it took her a moment to realize they were celebrating. She gave him a lacklustre high-five, and Chase cursed himself for not noticing sooner that she wasn't into the game.

"What's wrong?"

"Nothing. Just tired. It's been a long week." She shivered and he cursed under his breath that he hadn't noticed sooner that she wasn't well.

Chase pressed a hand to her forehead. "Just tired, my ass. You're burning up. Come on, I'll get you home."

"It's nothing."

"Sure. Bed."

"But Stella—"

Chase looked over at her friend, who waved them off. "I'll get someone else to drop me off, it's fine. Besides, I'm looking forward to kicking Beth's butt at Settlers. At least twice."

Chase bit back a smile at the barely suppressed matching groans from Ty and Finn. He had a valid excuse to get out of Dodge. They were on their own.

— —

Mari never got sick. This wasn't happening.

Except the next thing she knew, Chase was pulling up in front of her apartment, so she must have fallen asleep as soon as he piled her into his truck. "I'm just tired," she protested again as he opened her door.

"I can't carry you," he said quietly, stroking her cheek. "Not up the stairs, it's not safe. But I can get you to the door and help—"

"Oh for Pete's sake." She took a deep breath, which hurt from the tops of her thighs all the way to her shoulders. "I can get myself inside. Thank you for the drive home." She turned and wiggled her feet for the running board. *Man, she was bone tired.*

A solid wall of man chest met her as she tried to stand up. "Easy there," he whispered, holding on to her hips. "I'm coming up."

"You'll be terribly disappointed to discover that I'm just going to bed, alone."

He laughed. "You could never disappoint me."

Well, damn. That managed to warm her from the inside out.

At the door he took the key from her shaking hand and ushered her upstairs, a hand on her hip the entire way. And when she wobbled on the top step, he was right behind her, all hard and stable and yummy-smelling.

"Did you go swimming today?" she asked, as she rested her head back against his shoulder for a minute.

"Why?" He reached past her and turned the interior doorknob.

"You smell good. I like it when you wear sunscreen."

"I'll remember that," he said dryly. "In we go."

"I'm good," she protested weakly.

"You're delirious with fever. I'm going to find you some medicine, then tuck you into bed."

She shrugged, too tired to argue, and kicked off her shoes. She stumbled to her bedroom, Chase following slowly behind. A narrow strip of floor led from the door to her dresser and closet. The rest of the small room was taken up by her bed, which she of course knew, but Chase must not have been expecting, because when she stopped, he almost ran into her.

"I need to get changed," she whispered over her shoulder, her throat too hot and scratchy to speak any louder.

His breath brushed across her cheek. "We've made out with you wearing nothing more than a bathing suit. I'm helping you into bed."

His words managed to make their way past the viral haze she was cloaked in to light a spark inside her. *Damnit, why did she have to be sick?* His hands slid around her waist and popped the button on her jeans. She shivered under his touch, and he mistook it as a chill because he pressed a reassuring kiss to her temple and pulled her back against his chest. He pulled the zipper, then wiggled his thumbs under her waistband and pushed her jeans down her hips.

"These skinny jeans are hot as fuck, Mari, but not convenient when you've got a fever. Sit."

He kneeled in front of her and first pulled off her socks, then her jeans, one leg at a time. She leaned back, bracing herself on her hands, and tried to think of a way she could stave off being sick long enough to take advantage of having Chase between her bare legs. When she blinked and realized she was flat on her back and Chase was looming over her, concern etched all over his face, she admitted that wasn't going to happen.

"I'm sick," she rasped miserably.

"I know, sweetheart. Under the blankets." He rolled her

to the side, then back again, this time under her duvet. She whimpered as she fought to keep her eyes open, but he seemed to understand. She heard a gentle rustling that must have been him taking off his own jeans, because the last thing she felt before she drifted off was Chase sliding into bed behind her, his warmth surrounding her and his hand sliding over her hair.

# CHAPTER THIRTEEN

Once Mari slipped into a deeper sleep, Chase reluctantly climbed out of her bed, put his jeans back on, and headed out, snagging her keys as he left. He'd checked out her medicine cabinet, and her only bottle of ibuprofen was six months past its expiry date.

He drove the twenty minutes into the city, to the twenty-four hour pharmacy in an outer suburb, worrying about her the whole time. He picked up a bag full of pharmaceuticals and herbal bath salts, because Mari seemed like the type of girl who'd like those, then he went through the grocery section and found everything he'd need to make breakfast.

Whatever Mari had done this week, it had been too much. Or he'd been too much, dragging her to Arizona to play his girlfriend in some misguided attempt to be a man. A real man would know what his girlfriend had going on in her life that she needed to disappear for a few days.

*She's not really*—He silenced his inner critic. Their relationship might be unconventional, and Mari might not be a fan of labels or obligations, but whatever she was, it was real.

He quietly let himself back into her apartment, tucked the groceries away, put some of the drugs in her bathroom and the others on her dresser, and crawled right back into bed with her.

She stirred just long enough to give him a confused, bleary look, then fell fast asleep again with a single stroke of her hair. *If only she was so pliable when well.*

A few hours later she woke up coughing, she didn't even

blink when he handed her a glass of water and two different cough syrups. She just shrugged, took a shot of the purple one, and tucked into his shoulder.

Chase couldn't remember the last time he'd slept with someone wrapped around him. Kelly hadn't been a cuddler. There'd been a Suns cheerleader early in his Phoenix days who'd liked to sleep in a pile, but just as often she'd want one or two other people in that pile, so they hadn't worked out. And between the two women...a shockingly long seven years of one-night stands, the vast majority of which hadn't lasted all night. It had been easier that way.

That's what he'd said he wanted from Mari—an easy, no-strings attached excuse to get out of his parents' house. Well, off their property, anyway. And she'd agreed. Too readily, when he thought about it.

*She really doesn't want a relationship right now.* She was him, at the start of his career. But the idea of Mari hopping from casual affair to casual affair for the next ten years turned his stomach.

Not because she didn't have a right to enjoy herself—but because he'd be on the sidelines, watching. Waiting. *Hating.*

"You're thinking awfully hard," Mari croaked. He blinked at her, surprised that he could see her so clearly. The tall, unadorned window in the corner of her room bathed them in a silky grey light. He'd been thinking so hard he'd missed both the crack of dawn and her waking up. "Hey. Why are you in my bed?"

"You're sick." He propped himself up on one arm and frowned at her. What did she expect him to do, drop her off and head home?

"And you wanted an up-close and personal transfer of germs?"

He snorted. "I see you're feeling better."

"I crashed hard, holy crap."

"Are you hungry?" He pressed the backs of his fingers to her forehead. "You're still warm, but not as hot as last night."

"My throat hurts, I don't know about food."

"Tea?"

"Would you?"

He rolled his eyes and slowly climbed out of bed. Mari needed to spend more time with decent people.

— —

Mari stretched her aching arms over her head and rolled onto her side. Chase had his back to her and he was already stepping into his jeans. She snuck a peek at his legs and butt before they were wrapped in denim again. Long, strong legs. Long. Really long. And a tight butt that looked custom-made for biting.

She flopped onto her back and pressed her hand to where his had just been. She was clearly still feverish, no matter what he said.

He turned around, doing up his top button, but his hands froze there as his gaze raked across her body. She'd kicked off the blanket without thinking about the fact she was just in her top and panties. Oh well. Mildly Feverish Mari thought this was just fine as well.

"It's a damn shame you're not feeling well," he said quietly, his eyes finally meeting hers.

"I don't know—I like how you've been playing doctor so far…" Her suggestive purr would have had more oomph if it wasn't then interrupted by a coughing fit.

Chase backed up, bumping into the too close wall. "Tea. I'm making you tea. Then putting you in the shower— alone—and tucking you back into bed. Then I'm going to give you some space."

She pulled her blankets up to her neck and pouted.

Chase laughed. "Not too long, I promise." He gave her a long, hot look before he disappeared to the kitchen.

Jeez. Pass out next to a guy for a night and the boundaries all tumble away. Her stomach flip-flopped. This was a good thing. Inevitable after Arizona. So why did she feel a healthy dose of panic mixed in to the anticipatory lust?

Two minutes later, he brought her a tray with a cup of tea, a small carton of milk, a few sugar cubes in a dish, a bottle of Tylenol and a cranberry muffin.

"I didn't know how you took your tea. I also bought a lemon…"

She pushed herself up to sit, making sure the blanket still covered her bare legs. "Just milk. Wow. Thank you."

"You force-feed me enough cranberry stuff at the bar, I figured this was safe."

She grinned. "They're a good source of vitamin C."

He grunted and stepped back from the bed. "Forgot a spoon, be right back."

Mari looked at her tray. She wanted some butter for her muffin, but there was no way she could lift her voice long enough to call out for Chase. She set the tray aside, pulled on a pair of sweatpants, and padded after him.

"Butter," she said guiltily when he gave her a disapproving look.

"Sick," he said reproachfully in return. "Let me take care of you for, like, ten minutes."

"See? I'm feeling better already," she said, twirling on the spot. Okay, it might have made her a little lightheaded, but she managed to mask that as he caught her and pulled her close.

"So. About us." He caught his lower lip between his teeth and pinned an intent-laden look on her. "What are you doing tomorrow night?"

Happiness bloomed in her chest. This was worth getting out of bed for. "Nothing."

He crowded her against the kitchen counter in a slow, delicious way. "How about I bring over a pizza for dinner? Or we could go out?"

Pizza on her couch—her private, soft, comfortable couch—sounded perfect. "Yes. Bring it here."

He leaned in for a quick kiss.

"Not what I meant." She smiled. "But I'll take it."

"Now into the shower and back to bed for you. I'm going to leave before you get in the shower or I'm afraid I won't be able to stop myself from taking advantage of you."

"Do it," she whispered, her pulse fluttering like mad in her neck.

He groaned and lifted her up onto the counter, then nudged his way between the vee of her legs. "Give me a hug, woman. Then I'm going to leave you alone for thirty hours. You need your rest."

"I don't," she protested.

He tugged her to the edge of counter, close enough that she could feel how much he wanted her. "I think once we get started, we'll need all the energy we can muster."

She kissed his neck and squeezed her legs around his hips. "Maybe bring protein bars with that pizza."

— —

He thought that he'd escaped the Miller Inquisition when he made it home and into his loft without running into anyone. But after a few hours sleep, he got a text message from Audrey. **Karen's here. Mom wants you to grill some steaks for lunch.**

He hopped into the shower, threw on a t-shirt and shorts, and wandered over to the main house.

"I was summoned?"

Audrey was perched on a stool at the raised counter, shucking cobs of corn. "Correction. She wants you to grill *and* make a salad."

"What's she doing?"

"Recovering from thirty-five years of parenting three demanding offspring?"

"Four." He pointed at her as he grabbed a cutting board.

"Nuh-uh. I'm delightful. The happy surprise. The one that practically raised herself. No trouble at all."

"Maybe not for *Mom*."

She grinned. "So...earlier. Was that the country version

of the walk of shame? Rolling your pick-up truck silently up to the loft at seven in the morning?"

"Maybe I was just trying to be considerate to my still-sleeping family."

"No such luck. I got up and drove Dad to work so I could have his car today. First night you've slept over at Mari's."

He stiffened. He hadn't thought about that—not that they'd care he was gone, he was thirty-three, he could sleep wherever he damn well pleased, but that they'd noticed before that he *hadn't* been sleeping over.

"You've finally fallen into her heart, eh?"

He scowled at her. "Don't be melodramatic."

She popped a crouton into her mouth. "I'm not. Mari's famous for not letting guys sleep over."

Fuck, he didn't want to think about guys *not sleeping* with his...his...*Fuck.*

"That is not the face of a man who got laid last night."

"Give me those. They're for the salad, not your personal snack." He snatched the cellophane bag from her hands and scowled again. "You're not old enough to talk about getting laid."

She leaned in. "I'm just two years younger than your girlfriend, dude."

"Two crucial, virginal years."

She laughed. "I am *so* not a—"

"Mom!" Chase turned his head toward the living room. "Audrey spilled wine on your white tablecloth!"

"Asshole," she muttered. "Did not," she hollered just as loudly. "He just doesn't want me to talk about my sex life."

From the front room they heard laughter, then Karen wandered in rubbing sleep from her eyes. "You guys are loud. I was taking a nap."

"Tell your sister she should save herself for marriage."

"Can't do it. Sex is too wonderful."

Audrey snickered.

"No." Chase shook his head. "She thinks sex is

wonderful because it gave her a baby. It'll just give you heartache. Or a baby, which at your age is pretty much the same thing."

Karen crossed the room and snagged the bag of croutons, purposefully bumping him off centre with the growing bump that housed said baby. "Audrey, do you need a lecture about birth control?"

Chase frowned at his love-drunk older sister. "Safe sex is more than just birth control."

"Ooookay," Audrey stretched out the word as she waved her hands in the air. "You have managed to sufficiently buzzkill any inkling I might have had about sex. I'll go join a nunnery. Now finish making the damn salad." She turned to Karen, who tossed her a crouton. "Feeling better after your nap?"

They talked about pregnancy stuff for a few minutes, then as if he wasn't there, Audrey casually returned to the topic of him and Mari—this time, excluding him from the conversation.

"Have you noticed how Chase has changed in the last few weeks?"

"I know." Karen sighed melodramatically. "For a while there I thought he'd given up his man card for good."

He lifted his brow, but they pretended to ignore him, so he went back to chopping onions and cucumbers.

Audrey clapped her hands for another crouton, and Chase went to the cupboards in search of something else that might add crunch to the salad. "He used to be such an alpha male." She made a grunting noise, which dissolved into a giggle. "Now look at him. Making us salad."

"Lots of chefs are big, burly men," he muttered.

Karen made a contemplative noise. "But he's manly in other ways. Maybe Mari's given him a reason to be all alpha all over again."

Chase tapped his knife on the cutting board. "You're talking about me like I'm not even here."

Audrey grinned. "Would you rather we talk about you

when you're not here?"

"Isn't that a given? This salad needs bacon." He opened the fridge.

"Well, duh. To the bacon, and the talking. But it's not nearly as much fun now that I don't get any Google Alerts for you."

"You have Google Alerts set up for me? That's creepy."

"Your name, Kelly's name, Wardham, the West brothers—"

"The West brothers?" Chase looked over at Karen for verification that this was concerning behaviour, but she just grinned.

Audrey propped her hands on her hips. "What? They're excellent businessmen. And hot. I might go to work for them when I get back."

"You scare me."

"Good." She gave a pleased nod. "I think that means I'm doing something right."

"Dare I ask why you stalk my ex on Google?"

"She's a psycho hosebeast, that's why. I like to keep tabs on all threats."

"And what other threats are facing you right now?"

"Well, you running serious interference on my sex life for one…" She cackled and leapt off her bar stool. "Lunch almost ready? I'll go fetch Dad, he said he'd be done by noon."

He just shook his head as she darted out the door. But when he looked back at his older sister, she was beaming. "What?"

"It's so good to have you guys home again. My life was so quiet when you were in Arizona and she was at university."

"And now she's going overseas for a year. She's going to come back in love with some ex-pat English twit."

"As long as she comes back, that's all I care about."

They fell into an easy silence as they set the table, then Chase took the steaks out to the grill. A few minutes later his father stepped onto the deck.

"You look good there, son."

Chase grunted.

"How goes the search for your own deck and barbecue?"

"Nothing has excited me yet. I'm in no rush to move out."

His dad leaned on the railing and looked out at the lake. "Pretty soon it'll be too cold to swim. Have you thought about getting back on skates this winter?"

Chase took a deep breath. "That's not going to happen."

"For fun, I mean."

He turned sharply, meat forgotten. "You're not upset?"

Hank frowned. "Why would I be upset?"

"Because I'm done with hockey." Not really. He wanted to be back on skates, just without any expectations. "And I haven't done anything about that."

"You've been talking to Dr. Mettner."

"She's not really a sports psychologist. I mean she is, but that's not her area of expertise."

"I know. She's been helping you deal with your depression."

Shit. Now he felt like a shmuck. "I didn't realize you…"

"Sometimes I listen when your mother talks. Most of the time, actually. She's smart." Chase stared at his dad, who just turned back to the lake. "Did you hear that Davis is heading to Germany next week?"

Chase turned down the flame and closed the lid, then joined his dad at the railing. "Yeah, he told me. Sounds like it'll be a tough tourney, but his girls are good. Did you see the new uniforms for Team Canada?"

Hank laughed and bumped against his shoulder. "Silver lining of your career being over—not having to worry about wearing that god-awful design."

And just like that, something shifted in Chase's chest, and he breathed deeper and more easily than he had in ages.

# CHAPTER FOURTEEN

What should one wear for pizza, a movie, and probable sex?

Mari stood in front of her dresser holding black lace panties in one hand and a cotton "Monday" days of the week pair in the other. This was Chase, of the 1996 Essex Fair t-shirt. The man was two months past needing a haircut. Her underwear probably didn't matter. She'd be better off spending some time figuring out how she was going to guard her heart instead.

Oh god. Maybe they shouldn't have sex. Yet.

They should definitely have sex *soon*. But now that her fever had passed, clarity had set in. *Fearful* clarity.

Chase wasn't like the other guys she'd slept with. For one thing, he was bossy. And maybe he'd be like that in the bedroom, too, but that wasn't her worry. No, that would be just fine. Her fear was that she wasn't in charge. He might be waiting for her to pull the starter's pistol, but once they took that step, he wouldn't let her go.

And Mari didn't do relationships. Not even with surprisingly kind, gruff men who go out in the middle of the night to buy her cough syrup. Men who make her feel wanted at the height of illness and then restrain themselves because it's the right thing to do. Chase. Underneath his brittle exterior, he was such a good guy.

A keeper kind of guy.

A distracting kind of guy.

Maybe they should stick to being friends with *most* of the benefits.

He'd left her apartment yesterday morning and she'd

twirled her sick butt right into the shower, thinking about how good it felt to have him pressed up against her. How *right*. Then she'd slept most of the day, waking up just to medicate from the wide selection Chase had stocked her with, then drifting right back to the yummy dreams featuring a handsome, and half-naked NHL nursemaid.

Yep, they definitely needed some boundaries. Even today, when she'd been feeling so much better, and had spent most of the day playing her guitar, her mind had floated back to him time and again.

She'd tried to work on "Pedal to the Metal," but a different refrain kept floating through her head. *Because you're gruff, boy/Not a forever boy*. It didn't really apply to Chase. If she was being honest, it was more about herself than anyone else. And she couldn't quite put her finger on any other lyrics, or a general image she was going for. Just those two lines, so finally she'd picked up her guitar again and started picking. Maybe if she had the music down, the lyrics would come. Not her usual process, but she still thought of herself as a baby musician in so many ways.

Jerking her attention back to the present, and the question at hand, she took a deep breath and tossed the lace away. Not tonight.

Black yoga pants—the expensive ones that did good things for her butt—and a cute graphic t-shirt completed the "let's just make out" outfit.

She'd told him to come over any time after six. He knocked at five minutes to the hour.

"You're early," she teased as she swung open the door at the top of the stairs. She'd left the downstairs door unlocked for him.

"Eager," he said with a grin as he stepped inside, flooding her senses with the sight and smell and sound of *man*. Deep voice. Faint hint of coconut. Big, broad, golden-tinged giant in her space, who was *eager* to spend time with her. She pressed a hand to her quivering tummy and offered him a small smile.

He had an extra-large pizza box in one hand and a mix-and-match six pack from the liquor store in the other. He pressed a quick kiss to her forehead as he stepped inside. "I didn't know what you liked, so I got a couple of beers, some cider, and a cooler."

"They're all good."

He set dinner down on the table then came back to the door, toed off his boots and pulled her close. "You're all good, too?"

She nodded. "Much better. Thank you for taking care of me the other night."

He rested his gaze on her mouth. "No thank you required."

"Not even a kiss?" she whispered, tipping her head back in invitation.

He smiled, already lowering his mouth to hers. "I keep telling you you've got this backwards, Beadie." She felt his stubble first, that soft prickly warning that something awesome was about to happen to her lips. He sucked in a breath just before he kissed her, and the cool pull of air away from her skin made her head spin.

One of his hands smoothed down her back, curving around her body to cup her hip and press her pelvis into his. He was doing that whole body kissing thing again, and she let herself get lost in it.

When they broke apart, they were both breathing hard.

"So. Hungry?" Chase nodded sideways to the pizza as he rubbed a hand over his mouth.

"Yep," Mari breathed, and they both laughed. "For pizza," she added, moving to the kitchen to grab some napkins. "And maybe more kisses later on."

He just lifted one brow, as if to say *maybe?* A shiver made her tighten up all over, and she took a moment to compose herself before stepping back into the living room, where Chase was still waiting for her with that look on his face.

The look that said there was no maybe about it, and it wouldn't just be kissing. "I'm starving," he said quietly. "But

I can wait until you're ready to eat."

"It's not just one night of pizza," she whispered, her gaze locked on his.

"Sure it is."

*Lies.* Maybe he believed that, but he wasn't on the receiving end of that look. "Let's eat pizza—for real—and watch a movie."

He shrugged and stepped back, his posture relaxing. "What are the movie options?"

"Comedy or action?"

"No horror?" He laughed at the look on her face, which she hoped was a slightly less turned-off version of how she really felt about that suggestion. "Comedy, then."

"Scary movies are such a cheap way to get girl to cuddle up close. I'll do that no matter what." She thought about her DVD collection. "*The Hangover? Dodgeball? Identity Theft?*"

"All good. I vote *Identity Theft.*"

She grinned. "Good choice. Maybe next time you can choose a horror movie."

"Really?" He pointed to the pizza box, then the coffee table, and she nodded.

"No, not really. But keep on believing."

"Wicked woman."

She got the movie set up, then they settled in. After they each ate a few slices of the loaded pizza, Chase tugged her close. Their sides pressed together from knee to chest, and on her outside arm, his fingers were tracing lazy circles. Sparkling awareness shimmered throughout her entire body. This was *nice.* Like, simple boy + girl kind of nice. Two people with undeniable attraction, no drama, and an entire night to touch each other.

She slowly turned her head, surreptitiously breathing him in.

"I didn't go swimming today." His voice rumbled through his chest.

"No?" She pressed her forehead into his shoulder to hide her flaming cheeks. So much for the subtle sniff.

"I did put on a dab of sunscreen before I left, though. Just for you." His laugh started deep in his belly, reverberated through his entire body, and was adorably contagious. She started laughing too, and when she caught her breath and lifted her gaze to his, she swallowed hard at the desire there. "Come here," he whispered roughly, and she scrambled into his lap, movie abandoned.

He laced his fingers into her hair, holding her head as they kissed.

This kiss was hard, fast and punishing. Needy. Unbelievably hot. Her thighs clenched at his hips as her sex swelled and flooded in anticipation. *We'll do other stuff,* she promised herself. *No one's going home without an orgasm tonight.*

Ever so slowly, Chase dropped his hands down her back, both of them, to cup her bottom. He groaned as she arched her back, pressing her generous backside into his hands. "I love your ass," he said, nipping at her bottom lip. He squeezed and slid his hips between her legs, bringing the ridge of his erection to exactly the right spot. "Is this okay?"

She blinked slowly, her heartbeat like thunder in her ears. "Just like that…" she trailed off on a breath, then gasped as he rolled them together again.

He kept his hands anchored on her butt, like he'd found a safe harbour and didn't want to risk making another move. So she made one instead, reaching between them to slide her hands under his t-shirt. "I love your abs," she whispered, echoing his compliment. Under her fingertips, his muscles rippled as he flexed and she hummed appreciatively. "I've been thinking about this since you unzipped that wetsuit. Touching you here…"

"Do we need to slow down?" His voice was low and rough, but he sounded calm. In control. Not at all like his heat was a runaway freight train like hers.

"Uhm…" It was too hard to think when he was moving against her like that. It made her think of how good it would feel to have him beneath her naked, of feeling him thrusting inside her.

"Come here," he whispered, shifting sideways on the couch. She followed him down, shoving his t-shirt up his torso at the same time, but as he swung his legs up to stretch out, he let out a strangled cry.

Mari froze. Had she hurt him somehow? Beneath her, he'd tensed up from head to toe. Sexy mood forgotten, she scrambled off of him as delicately as she could manage and stood there beside the couch for a moment before finding her voice. "Are you okay?"

"I'm fine," he muttered through clenched teeth, his words strained.

"Do you...hum...what can I do?"

"Nothing." His eyes were closed, and he slowly blinked them open. "Seriously, I'm fine."

"Right. You sound fine."

He shot her a black look and she lifted her hands. "Hey, snarky gets you snarky back."

He huffed an almost laugh. "It's just my leg, sometimes it cramps up."

"Can you take your pants off?"

"I knew you were just waiting until I was debilitated to admit you can't resist me, Beadie."

"I've already admitted that, Miller." But it wasn't her goal at the moment. "I've got something that works wonders. Be right back."

She hopped up and dashed to the bathroom, grabbing the glass jar of her mother's special blend of essential oil salve. Back in the living room, Chase was still lying on the couch, his legs stiff and straight. His head was tipped back and his eyes were clenched shut. And he hadn't taken off his pants.

*Don't molest him*, she cautioned herself. She settled one hand gently on his thigh. Hard, twisted muscles pressed against her palm. "Pants?" she asked quietly.

He made a *go ahead* gesture, and she reached for the button. "We keep meeting like this," she joked lamely, but he didn't respond. Two nights before it had been his turn to undress her in unsexy conditions. Maybe it was the universe's way of saying they shouldn't take things to the next level.

Although it was hard to imagine that was possible. Why would the universe deliver Chase to her if she weren't allowed to eventually have him?

She returned to her task. She'd spent weeks avoiding thinking about his fly, and what yumminess lay behind it, and she'd apparently done such a good job of that she hadn't noticed that he wore button-fly jeans. The teenage girl inside her made a squealing sound. The responsible adult sadly noted that his jeans were loose enough that she didn't need to actually undo each of those tempting buttons. And his erection had faded, so groping him while he was in pain would just be creepy. "Lift," she murmured, and with a tug his jeans were sliding down his legs.

Seeing him in boxer-briefs on her couch was pretty much the same as swim trunks in the pool, although those had been longer. And not fitted. His at-rest package was still pretty captivating. *Focus.* The poor guy was stiff as a board and white as a sheet. This wasn't the time to drool over his physical perfection.

"Which leg is it?" she asked, opening the jar. She didn't need to ask, not really. His left leg was a maze of scars, although given all the surgeries he'd been through, it still looked remarkably like the right one. Just...decorated. She took a deep breath and dipped her fingers into the salve. The oil warmed and slicked over her fingers instantly. She pressed her hand just above his knee, the light brown hair on his legs crinkling under her touch. But beneath that furry dusting lay hard, hot man flesh that made her heart rate pick up in the most inappropriate way. She took a steadying breath and stroked the oil up his thigh, curving the tingly medicine around the tense, ridged quadricep muscles.

"What the hell is that," he groaned, but his leg started to relax under her touch so she continued, following the scar tissue up his leg to where the muscles looked tightest.

"A liniment my mom makes up. It works wonders."

"Holy shit, no kidding." He tentatively arched his hip. "Can you go a bit higher?"

Was the pope Catholic? She bit her lip and thought of guitar chords as her fingers glided toward the bottom edge of his boxers.

"Why does your mom make her own sports rub?" Chase asked, his voice less tense than before.

Mari hesitated for a moment, but she couldn't hold back a little laugh. "Well…that's not really what she'd call it."

He opened one eye a crack and looked at her. "What would she call it?"

"My parents own a horse farm." She pressed her lips together and gave him her best *not a big deal* look.

He glanced down at her hand, now right at the top of his thigh, then back at her face. "Horse liniment."

"It works?" She shrugged, then smoothed her hand back down to his knee. "There. Better?"

He started to nod, then stopped. He looked at her hand again, and all of a sudden her apartment felt small. And hot. Chase shifted slightly, and she couldn't keep her gaze from wandering back to where he'd lost his arousal. And now…

"Higher again," he said, his gaze hooded.

She couldn't break eye contact—or skin contact. Not when he looked at her with such blatant hunger. She swallowed hard and slid her hand up his inner thigh.

"Higher." Her heart was pounding so hard she could barely hear the coarse instruction.

"The tingles might not be, uhm, you know. For sensitive skin," she whispered, her chest rising and falling rapidly as she toyed with the bottom of his boxers again. His erection jutted out from his body, tenting the black cotton, and she wanted more than anything to wrap her hand around him. Feel that hot, private skin against her hand. Jerk him off.

She gasped as he shoved his waistband low enough for her to see where his cock sprouted.

"Use your other hand." His voice was oh so thick, like

molasses, and his words wound around her in a hypnotic web.

She reached forward with her ointment-free hand and traced the exposed inch of his shaft with her fingertips. "What are we doing?" she asked in a whisper.

"Just what feels good. Whatever you're comfortable with."

She nodded. Oh boy did it feel good. Hot velvet and throbbing man. She still hadn't seen all of him, but at the root he was bigger, thicker than anyone else she'd been with. Of course he was. Chase Miller was sex on a stick and he knew it. It was a wonder they hadn't done this sooner.

"Can I touch you?" Both of his hands were still tugging down his boxers, but his eyes were already touching her all over.

She shook her head. "One crazy step at a time, Miller." God, she couldn't tear her eyes away from the almost-look she was having at his naked cock. She licked her lips. "We need some boundaries."

He laughed, a strained, painful sound. "Like the just kissing thing?"

She closed her eyes. Okay, so she was just delaying the inevitable. But damn it, she *needed* the delay. "Will you laugh if I say we can do everything but?"

"Everything but...intercourse?"

"Yes."

He glanced to her mouth, then back to her eyes. It was a weird conversation to be having when she could have her hand wrapped around him instead, she'd grant him that much, but to his credit, he didn't seem annoyed. Just...cautious. "Is this about feelings?"

*Not if I can help it.* She blew a derisive raspberry. "Oh, come on. Maybe yours."

"You prefer the friends with benefits thing." He said it like a statement, carefully and without any clue if that was good or bad.

"Yes!" The affirmation burst out of her faster than she

expected. "It's…smart. And I think not doing *something*, keeping that one thing off limits, might help us remember what we're doing here. And what we aren't doing."

"Feelings." He didn't sound totally convinced, but she ignored that.

"Exactly." She stroked him again, this time reaching into his briefs. She was rewarded with a groan, which justified ignoring the feelings conversation. That groan pleased her to her core. "So tonight maybe I'll touch you. And tomorrow you could touch me."

"That doesn't work for me," he muttered, his eyelashes fluttering shut. "If I come on your hand, you're going to come on mine. Tonight. Right here. Maybe twice."

Okay, that worked too. But she couldn't let him have the upper hand. He could so easily have it all the time, so he'd need to work for it now. "We'll see."

She'd felt him between her legs how many times now? And yet she was shaking as he dragged his briefs lower still until her entire hand, wrapped firmly around his shaft, was exposed. Then there was his crown, shiny and wet, and her mouth watered.

And the rules went out the window.

He might have said something, or just groaned, but she wasn't really listening. All she could think about was that drop of pre-come swelling on his tip and how much she wanted it on her tongue. She licked it up, the burst of his unique taste only confirming how deep her hunger for him ran. Another lick, then another, until she'd thoroughly loved the head of his cock and needed more of him in her mouth. She swallowed him deep, loving the sounds he made, the way his legs moved restlessly against her shoulders and how his hands danced around her head.

With her free hand, she reached up and pressed his palm more firmly against her hair. *Show me*, she told him with her touch. *Show me how deep you want to be inside me. Show me what you want and I'll give it to you. Or just take it. I'm yours to take.*

He groaned again as he clenched his ass, thrusting

himself into her mouth, and then both his hands were tangled in her hair as he set a jerky, shallow rhythm. He started whispering to her, at first words about how it felt—good, wet, hot—and then what he wanted her to do. "Swirl your tongue. Lick me, Mari. Oh, jeez, yes, lick me there. Keep that up and I'm going to come on your talented little tongue."

That made her moan, and she scrambled her lower body into a better position between his legs so she could use her hand in tandem with her mouth to help bring him to the brink. When he eased his grip on her head, she slid a gaze toward his face just in time to see him tip his head back against the couch cushions. "Do it," she murmured triumphantly, then swallowed him again.

Two thrusts later, he did, and she took him as deep as she could, keeping him in her mouth until he was finished.

"Now see," he said wearily when she pressed her cheek against his thigh and smiled up at him. "This is why *I'm* the one who should be saying thank you to *you*."

She couldn't disagree with that. She had just blown his mind.

"Proud of yourself, eh?"

"Maybe a little bit."

His eyes softened and he rubbed his thumb over her lower lip. "Your mouth, sweetheart. Jesus, I like I like it even more than your ass."

She parted her lips and swiped at him with her tongue.

"Enough of that," he rasped. "Let me up."

Mari reluctantly pressed herself up on all fours and away from his addictive body. Chase pulled his shirt off, then stood, straightening his boxer briefs as he got up. He looked like an underwear model, with his long, muscular legs, tight hips and butt, and then the flare of his sculpted back up to his broad shoulders.

"Okay," he said, turning back to her.

"Okay, what?"

He gave her a slow, wicked grin. "Okay, your turn."

# CHAPTER FIFTEEN

It was positively indecent how good Mari looked spread out on her bed in nothing but a tiny white pair of panties with Monday stamped right above her pussy. Those were fucking hot, but he wasn't sure that was how they were intended, so he kept that reflection to himself for the time being.

He'd hauled her up off the couch and hustled her to the bed as soon as he got full feeling back after that incredible blow job. He wasn't going to be quick about this, and when they were done, he had every intention of going to sleep curled around her. Might as well make that move now before she was bonelessly post-orgasm. She'd giggled as he swatted her butt and ordered her out of those indecent yoga pants he liked so much, and sighed as he'd pressed her against the doorframe and peeled off her t-shirt between kisses.

Now he swallowed hard as he tracked his gaze over the sweet swell of her belly and the nip of her waist to the glorious roundness of her breasts. He held himself back from leaping on her and kept going, needing to check in with her. He found her watching him, her eyes hot and half-lidded.

"What do you want to do with me?" she asked huskily, tucking her fingertips under the waistband of the only scrap of clothing left between them.

"Everything but, sweetheart. Until you're begging me for everything. And even then, I'm going to make you wait for being a brat."

She bit her lip, but her eyes twinkled. "It'll be worth the

wait."

"I have no doubt." He picked up her nearest foot and slid her legs further apart, not missing how she arched her back. Soft curves and long, smooth stretches of skin. Shadows and light. He glided his rough hands up her calves, relishing the feel of her bare skin. She shivered when his fingertips grazed the underneath of her knees, and he circled back to that spot. She rewarded him with another shiver and a sigh as her eyelids fluttered shut. He leaned forward, and inside his boxers his cock leapt forward, wanting to beat the rest of him to the warmth between her legs.

He skated his left hand over her hips, pretending he couldn't feel the slight tremor in his arms, and braced his right forearm beside her head. "Open your eyes, Mari," he whispered, his mouth hovering right above hers.

"Kiss me instead," she teased, smiling even as she squeezed her eyes shut tighter.

"I like the look in your eyes when you're turned on. When *I* turn you on."

She blinked up at him. "There's a look?"

He grinned and kissed her, sucking her lower lip into his mouth before diving deeper with his tongue. "Yep. And it's hot as fuck."

"You have a dirty mouth."

"Not usually." But there was something about her that unleashed his primal side.

"Lucky me." Her chest rose and fell between them, two tempting peaks pressing into his skin. Lucky him.

He kissed his way down her neck, loving the way her breath hitched as he cupped her left breast. The soft, sweet flesh fit perfectly in his palm, and he nuzzled her skin, inhaling her scent before he sucked her nipple into his mouth. She cried out, flexing beneath him as he tugged more of her against his tongue. The rub of her erect nipple inside his mouth, contrasting with the impossible softness pressed against his lips…it was all too good. Too unbelievably, fuck him for being so damn lucky, amazingly good.

Mari wrapped her arms around his neck, holding him to her chest, and twisted her legs against his, urging him closer. Fuck, yes. He greedily made his way to her other breast, leaving his thumb in charge of keeping the first nipple happy, and when she started tugging on his hair, he couldn't hold off any longer. He lowered his weight onto her, and into her, her body moulding around his as he brought his mouth back to hers for a scorching kiss.

She whimpered into his mouth as he rocked his erection between her legs. She was slippery as fuck, even through two layers of cotton. "You going to come like this? Grinding against me, baby? You just sucked me off, and do you feel how hard I am? I'm a fucking rock, Mari. That's what you do to me."

She bit his lip not hard, but she wanted to. She was holding herself back. And he wanted her to fly.

"You want to bite me? Mark me? Do it." He stared down at her flushed face, her parted wet lips and her dark, flashing eyes. He wanted those eyes on him as she came for him. When he finally got under her skin the way she'd been living under his for weeks now. Because he was pretty sure that Mari still had some solid walls, and she was afraid they'd crack and fall away when he got close enough.

"Chase," she breathed, lifting her hips to meet his, and he wasn't sure that he wasn't going to come like this himself. He was pulling out all the stops, getting inside her head and painting filthy pictures, and all she had to do was breathe his name and his balls clenched tight.

"I want you naked," he growled. "I know the rules. But I need to feel how wet you are."

"No…" she sighed as he pulled away, and he stopped.

It was hard as hell, but he stopped. His heart rate slowed like he'd been conditioned to in the face of a difficult situation. "No?"

She shook her head rapidly. "Not no like stop, just no like don't stop. I mean….damnit, I can't think. Come back here."

He laughed and shucked his underwear, then reached for hers. "This is going to feel even better, sweetheart."

She grabbed at his wrists, holding his hands at her hips. "Chase…I'm going to beg you. And…."

"We won't." He licked his lips, willing himself to keep that promise. He would. "We're both going to want to, but not tonight."

She blinked slowly and dropped her hands to her side, her hands splaying wide against the mattress as she lifted her hips. He bared her in one soft tug, and her legs fell open. He was captivated by the dark triangle of hair topping her sex, and instead of climbing back on top of her, he dropped to his belly, sliding his near-granite cock into the most comfortable position he could find beneath him. Rutting against her would have to wait until he'd had a taste.

He pressed kisses first to one inside thigh, then the other. The scent of her swirled around him, and her wetness glistened, calling for his mouth. But he wanted to take his time, because it didn't feel real. They'd danced around this attraction between them for so long that he'd started to convince himself that they really were just playing, and one day soon Mari would just look at him and casually ask him to break up with her.

Charade over.

But there wasn't anything fake about this.

And his fear about *this* ending was so much bigger, so much scarier than losing the casual thing they'd been pretending to have. Because with Mari, he was a new man. A better man. And she wasn't interested in forever. Not that he was, necessarily. *Yes, you fucking coward. You want her forever.* Well, yeah. He wanted Mari forever. The thought of letting her go, seeing her with someone else…it made him insane. But he couldn't be a caveman. That wouldn't impress her. So he needed to take his time. Needed to convince her that he could be whatever she needed, whatever she wanted, whenever she wanted it.

And right now, she wanted to come.

He could deliver that at least a few times over.

— —

The first swipe of Chase's tongue between her folds was heaven. She closed her eyes and gave herself over to the best thing since...ever. The second was hell, because it wasn't enough. He'd pulled back, teasing her, and she lifted her hips in a wanton demand.

"More, Chase." She groaned and tipped her head back.

"You know what I want, Mari."

She grabbed her pillows and doubled them up behind her head. "Better?"

"Eyes on me, and I'll do this all night." He slid his hands under her hips, holding her in just the right place so he could suck her clit into his mouth and keep that hypnotic stare pinned on her at the same time.

Her eyelids were so damn heavy, but that just made it hotter, watching this big man go down on her through tunnel vision. All she could see was him. All she could feel was him. From the outside in, as he licked deeper, fucking her with his tongue, and then from the inside out as he swirled back up to her clit and pulled that fire he'd stoked right out of her.

She gasped his name as he sucked harder, and groaned when he slid one long finger inside. She could hear how wet she was as he added another digit, and when he lifted his face and gently blew on her clit at the same time as he surged inside her again with three fingers, she realized that she'd been foolish to think that this might fall short of everything.

Her entire body writhed under his touch as he found that special spot inside her and he flicked his gaze up to her, smiling slowly when he found her staring hotly back at him. "Come on my fingers, baby," he said roughly, twisting his hand.

She rocked her hips, looking for something against her clit. His thumb fell into place, then he dropped his head to her thigh and breathed in. And that was what did it. The rest was amazing, but that little inhale crumbled the last of her walls and she cried out as she came apart. Her knees pulled high up her body and her shoulders curled forward, but still she stared at him.

"That look, sweetheart," he whispered, slowly crawling up her body. "That's the look. Best thing ever."

She reached for him with shaking arms, pulled him down on top of her. She kissed him hungrily, tasting herself on his lips, then trailed her mouth across his jaw and down his neck. She really did want to bite him, and nipped at the corded tendon there as a test. He hissed and arched his back, but between them his cock flexed. She did it again, and he shoved his hips hard against hers. Emboldened, she pressed a hot, open-mouth kiss against the hot, flat skin stretched over the straining muscle just below his collarbone and dragged her teeth together. He rocked his erection through her wet folds.

Mari took a deep breath. The urge to tip her hips and pull him inside her was overwhelming.

"Don't," he growled, and she jerked her gaze up to his face. "Don't think about how good it would feel with me inside you." And then he grinned like a bastard who knew exactly what he was doing to her.

Two could play that dirty game. She licked her lips. "But it would," she panted, pressing herself against the length of him. "You'd fill me up."

"Jesus Christ, you're a wicked woman." He jerked between her legs, then smoothed his rhythm again. "Maybe no second orgasm for you."

"I can do it myself," she whispered, licking his collarbone to the other side of his neck. "Get my fingers busy."

"We'll do that next." And as if he wanted to make sure she waited, he pulled her hands from around his neck and pinned her against the bed. "Mari..." he trailed off, his face shifting away from the playful moment they'd just shared. Her breath caught in her throat at the seriousness—the heaviness—that draped around them. "This is..."

She rocked her hips and pulled her knees up high against his sides. "I know," she whispered.

"Do you?" He searched her face for something—reassurance? Commitment?

"This is real," she promised, and that seemed to hit the mark. He moved her hands closer together above her head and clasped them together lightly with one of his. The other he trailed down her cheek and onto her side. She arched her back, pressing their chests together. Was it gauche to promise a guy there really were feelings between them in one breath and beg him to suck your nipples in another?

"We've got all the time in the world, Mari," he said roughly, grinding against her. "But I'm done going slow for tonight."

They'd been going slow? Sweetness and light, she wasn't sure she could handle fast.

He gripped the back of her leg, opening her even wider, and then he thrust so firmly she had to think hard for a second to double check they weren't actually fucking. She gasped at the residual pulse deep inside, and then he did it again. And again. Until she couldn't keep her eyes open any longer, and it didn't matter because his head was buried in her neck, and they so closely entwined it was as if they were one.

When they exploded at almost at the same moment, the hot splash of Chase's release on her stomach driving her own orgasm, Mari felt an overwhelming perfection that made her want to cry. And when Chase touched her cheek, she realized that she actually was, which was mortifying.

He didn't say anything, just rolled off her and padded buck-naked to the bathroom, returning with a washcloth and a gentle smile. She brushed her tears away and took the cloth. She got the impression he'd wanted to clean her up himself, but was thankful for the unsexy but very grounding moment to herself. She scrambled off the bed, and followed the same path, dumping the washcloth in the hamper. She washed up, then grabbed another flannel to take back.

She found him tucked into her bed. *So we're not going to discuss a sleepover?* Probably fair enough after he'd slept next to her while she was sick. He still didn't say anything, just watched as she set the new cloth on the dresser and turned out the light, then lifted the blanket. He was still naked, beautifully so, and despite all the noise in her head—a lot of it unexpected—she still wanted to be close to him.

"We might need that in the middle of the night," she finally said after she'd cuddled tight to his big, hard body.

He laughed, a slow, rolling noise that warmed her to her core. "There's no might about it, sweetheart."

— —

Chase had no idea what time it was, but the sun was bright and Mari's bed was missing a warm, naked woman. They'd continue to fool around and just touch each other throughout the night, but they hadn't had a repeat of the emotional reaction from Mari. He hadn't minded it— frankly, he'd slept with enough women to know that sometimes tears happen after sex, although he sure as shit wasn't going to tell her that.

But unlike the awkwardness of tears in a casual hook-up, that moment of emotional nakedness had touched him in an unexpectedly positive way. A quiet victory for the hope of a future together, maybe.

He lay there for a minute, listening to the quiet, and then he heard the rustling of papers. Ah. So he wasn't totally abandoned. He rolled out of bed, snagged his boxers, and visited the bathroom to steal some toothpaste.

She started strumming her guitar as he finished up, and he stood in the hallway for a minute listening before his stomach rumbled. She glanced up as he walked in, and he flashed her a smile, but she looked like she was in the middle of something so he busied himself in the kitchen making use the breakfast supplies he'd bought and not used the other day.

Ten minutes later, Mari wandered her and wrapped her arms around him from behind. "Something smells good in here," she said, pressing a kiss to his spine. "And I like the look of you cooking for me in just your boxers, Miller."

He glanced back her. She was wearing snug yoga shorts and an oversized t-shirt, and looked pretty delectable herself. "Good morning." He let his gaze linger on her until his mushrooms demanded a stir. "Anything you don't like in an omelet?"

"Nope, I'm easy."

"And thank god for that," he muttered, then laughed as she elbowed him in the kidney.

"Hey, I held out as long as I could. You're pretty irresistible, though."

He bit the inside of his cheek to keep from grinning like a fool. "I am?"

"Oh, shut up with that *aw shucks* routine. You could seduce the pants off a nun."

"Nuns don't wear pants."

"Sure they do. Like a modern nun." She shrugged when he gave her a raised eyebrow look. "Let it go. My point is—"

He reached out and pulled her close, cutting her off. He turned down the vegetables and twisted to give her his full attention. Firmly. "I'm not seducing anyone. I'm waiting patiently and getting creative within the bounds allowed."

He watched her face as she bit back a snarky response, then stifled another one. Her eyes narrowed, then she licked her lips and tilted her head.

"Nope," he cut her off again, this time before she could even start. "Mari. It's just me. No games. We can just…be friends with benefits. Partial, full, whatever. Or we can be more. Whatever you want." That was a bald-faced lie. They could only be what they *were*, which was a hell of a lot more than friends. But he'd do his best to keep a lid on that realization if she wanted him to.

Her eyes flared wide, and for a moment he saw a glimpse of that same vulnerability from the night before. But she took a deep breath and just as quickly it was gone again. "Okay. Sorry," she muttered.

"No need to be sorry. I like the banter, I just don't want you to think you need to perform for me. And I'm not performing for you, or anyone else. This is me. Last night was real, not something I gamed out of you like a player."

She burrowed into his chest at that, and he stroked his hand over her hair. "Last night was real for me, too," she said quietly.

"I know, baby." God, she was skittish, even when she came to him.

"It's just that…I need to focus on this album. Now more than ever. So I don't know how much time I can give to us."

"I'm not asking for time. Well, maybe just a bit. Breakfast. Bedtime. A few stolen kisses in between. But you do what you've gotta do." She hugged him tighter, which he didn't know quite how to interpret. It wasn't a *bad* thing, anyway. "What do you mean, now more than ever?"

"Nothing." He waited. She waited, too, but not as long as he did. Finally she sighed into his chest and pushed back, leaning against the counter. She stared at her feet. "I went to Toronto for a thing and…" she continued, but the trailed off mumble was incomprehensible.

"Mari," he said quietly, drawing her attention back to his face. "You think I'm some hockey superstar. I'm really the guy who spent a decade not quite believing I'd made it to the NHL. Now I'm living over my dad's garage while I overcome depression. There's zero reason not to share whatever dirty secret you've got with me."

She rolled her eyes, but cracked a smile. "First of all, we need to work on that official rendering of your life, because whew, that's not how anyone else in the known universe would describe it. And no, it's nothing shameful." She took a deep breath. "I had an audition. Actually, a couple of them, in a row. And I didn't make the cut."

"Wow. That sucks." He grimaced. "Sorry."

"Yeah. No, it's fine. I don't want to sing other people's stuff anyway."

"That's what it would have been?"

Her cheeks turned pink.

"Out with it. What aren't you telling me?"

"I think that's enough sharing for one morning," Mari muttered, and moved as if to go around him.

He reached out his hand. "Hey, I'm making you an omelet in my underwear. We can't talk about this?"

"What happened to *I'm not asking for much, just a few kisses*?" Her eyes suddenly flashed angry. Not, not angry. Defensive.

He slowly lifted his hand, letting her pass. That wasn't exactly what he'd said. She stormed into the living room, and he took a deep breath. He had no right to her secrets. He hadn't earned them yet—and maybe he never would. He was no relationship expert.

*There's plenty she doesn't know about you.* But if she asked...

Chase turned back to his bowl of cracked eggs. Food first. Then they'd try again.

# CHAPTER SIXTEEN

How could she stay prickly when he brought her breakfast to the coffee table, kissed her head, said he was going to take a quick shower? Like she hadn't had a temper tantrum because he'd asked a simple question?

She wasn't even sure what she was mad about. The thought of admitting to Chase that she'd tried out for a reality show made her queasy. It was like highlighting the fact that she wasn't a real artist in bright neon yellow. She'd signed up months ago, and almost dropped out a bunch of times. But after their weekend in Arizona, Mari had decided to go for it. Lots of people were taking alternate paths to success these days, and she wasn't going to cut herself off from any of them.

Turned out she wasn't commercial enough. And for her three days of eighteen-hour practicing and performing marathons, being followed by intrusive video cameras most of the time, she got nothing but a stupid virus and a five hundred dollar honorarium.

There weren't any shortcuts to success. There was only hard work, serious craft, and random good luck. She couldn't control the last bit, but she could re-double her efforts in the first two arenas. And after the three days of filming and racing from one task to the next, she knew that a TV show wouldn't have been a shortcut either. Just hard work and craft in a different form.

Besides, "Gruff Boy" had taken on new meaning this morning, and her enthusiasm for the album renewed just like that. *An artist's mercurial temperament*, she reminded herself. She needed to stay the course and believe in herself.

Hard to do when her only tangible fan was Stella. She picked up her guitar and picked out the melody that felt like a part of her already.

"That sounds amazing," Chase said, padding back into her living room when she finished. He was now wearing more clothes and he'd grabbed his own breakfast. He sat on the far couch and watched her with that addictive *I'm interested* smile on his face. Maybe she had a second fan in Wardham after all.

"You like it?"

"I really do."

"It's a little bit inspired by you. Mostly not." She blushed. "Ignore I said that."

"Nope, can't do that. Now you have to start from the beginning." Just then, his phone rang. He hit ignore, but she could tell she'd lost his full attention.

"It's okay, I'll play it for you...tonight?"

He gave her a surprised look. "Yeah? I didn't want to assume."

"Yeah." They shared a private smile that gave her a dirty thrill. "I think we've blown those boundaries out of the water, anyway."

"We don't need to..."

She smiled, more coyly this time. "I know. But I want to."

He glanced at his phone and she laughed. "Not now! I want to finish this, and I've got a shift at Danny's tonight."

"What time are you getting off?"

She pressed her lips together, barely holding in a laugh.

He furrowed his brow for a second, then burst out laughing. "Right. Hopefully not long after you're done work?"

She winked. "I think we'll probably close at ten-thirty tonight, unless we're busy, then eleven."

He gobbled his breakfast, then took both plates to the kitchen and did a quick wash-up. When he came back, he leaned over the couch and kissed her cheek, lingering there for a moment. She turned her head more in his direction and he gave her a slow, light, sweet kiss on the lips for good measure.

"Until tonight, then," he said, pressing his forehead against hers.

That made two of them, and over the course of the day she thought about that kiss and the breakfast he made her. And before that, the sharp spike of fear that said, *don't make me go there. I don't want to share.* But Chase was a vault—his word, both for himself and for her. He valued privacy above almost all else.

Her secrets were safe with him.

She was safe with him. She pulled out her phone during a lull in bar service and sent him a text message.

**It was a reality show try-out. That's why I went to Toronto.**

His response was immediate. **Brave! Want to tell me more about it?**

**Maybe. Not now.**

**Did you know I was approached to be on Skating With the Stars a couple of years ago?**

**Hahaha. No. But you turned it down?**

**I had to. I get stage fright.**

Wow. Mr. Grumpy Pants was really Mr. Shy Pants? That was unexpected information.

Her phone beeped again. **Are you silently judging me? :P**

Okay, Chase had just used an emoticon. This might be the beginning of the end of days. She stuck her tongue out at her phone, and then pulled it back into her mouth. It was a good thing he couldn't see her. **Not at all. We'll share embarrassing stories later.**

**I'll be there at ten-thirty. I'll walk you home.**

She smiled and pressed her hand to her tummy. Damn butterflies. She could be cool about this. **K. Hey, I uploaded Gruff Boy to YouTube this afternoon.**

**Gruff Boy??? I missed the name before. Ha. Okay, I'll watch it in a bit.**

The rest of her shift flew by, and before she knew it, she was ushering the last of her patrons out the door.

And her favourite patron was sitting quietly on his regular stool, taking up way too much space in the empty bar. He spun around lazily, his gaze tracking her as she swayed back in his direction.

"Can I help you sweep up?" His grin transformed his face, and she stepped into the vee of his legs, unable to resist touching his happy face. He wrinkled his brow at her. "What?"

"You used to be the grumpiest man in Wardham."

"Rumour has it I'm getting laid tonight. And I got laid last night. And if I play my cards right, this might be a good thing for me. A regular, happy-making thing."

"Regular?" She liked the sound of that.

"What do you say? Want to be my girlfriend?"

She folded against him, bringing her lips to his ear. "You keep propositioning the bartenders in here. And I hear you have a harem."

"I'm incorrigible. But I sweep your floors." He twisted and kissed her neck. "And I'll toss in a neck rub when we get to your place."

She sighed a happy sigh and tipped her head back, inviting more of those nipple-tingling neck kisses. He did not disappoint, either in turning her on or in helping tidy up in record fashion.

"What did you do today?"

Chase wrapped his arm around her for the short walk from the bar to her apartment. That casual brush of his warm body against hers felt like pure electricity. She wanted to rub against him and absorb more of it. Stock it up for when the inevitable end came.

"House hunting with my mom. It was a bust, I might end up building if I can find some land I like." They stopped in front of her door and he gave her a bit of space to unlock, but his hands never left her body. They headed upstairs. "But hey…I got a call from the transport company and my cars will arrive next week."

"That's fun," Mari said, hanging her keys on their hook.

"You know what else is fun?" Chase asked, his breath hot and intoxicating against her cheek.

"We're alone?"

He flashed a grin in the periphery of her vision. "And my beautiful girlfriend has finally done away with boundaries and rules."

She needed to not pass out before they actually made love. "I did," she said softly, turning to face him fully. That was a good call. Chase full-on was reassuring. Serious. Warm. Wanting.

Oh jeez, the look in his eyes. That would fuel her fantasies forever. Eyelids at half-mast, pupils dilated, and his hot gaze fixed on her face. "I want you so much, Mari. I had no idea what I was starting with that kiss, but I thank Christ I did it because you make me…" He squeezed her waist, sliding his hands underneath her shirt.

She glided her hands up his biceps to his straining shoulder muscles. He was holding himself back, and that wouldn't do. Chase's restraint was a big part of why she'd fallen hard for him, but it wasn't necessary tonight. "What do you want to do with me?"

His thumb stroked back and forth over her bottom rib, making her shiver. "Get naked, for starters. Stay that way all night. Get you wet, over and over again, and when you're squirming hard for my cock, I'm going to give it to you. Over and over again."

While he talked, she'd wound her arms around his neck, and at the visual of finally having Chase deep inside her, she gave a little hop and hoisted herself up onto him, wrapping her legs around his waist.

"That's a neat trick," he growled, turning to press her against the wall. "I knew you were flexible, but that was cheerleader-esque."

She narrowed her gaze at him teasingly. "I bet you know all about cheerleaders."

— —

There it was again, that little defensive wall. His first instinct was crude, that maybe he could fuck that out of her, but that wasn't the right order of things. He pinned her tighter against the wall with his hips and ran his hands up the inside of her shirt, cupping her breasts. She tipped her head back, thudding it against the wall as he thumbed over her nipples.

"The only woman in my head and under my skin is you," he rasped. "Is that clear?"

"Crystal," she panted.

"Do we need to talk about our histories?" He ground their hips together and lowered his head to suck gently on her neck.

"No." She swallowed, her throat working under his mouth.

"You're the only woman I want in my bed." *Ever again*, but he knew better than to add that.

"Well, so far it's only been my bed," she said, gasping at the end when he pinched her right nipple.

"You have such a smart mouth," he muttered, licking along the ridge of her collarbone. He needed to put her down before his leg cramped up, but this was too much fun.

She smirked. He couldn't see it, but he could damn well feel it against the top of his head. "You liked my mouth just fine last night."

"I fucking loved your mouth last night. And actually, that's a great idea." He jerked his hips against her one more time, then stepped back. She instinctively let go of his waist and stepped onto the floor. He laughed and pressed one hand firmly onto her shoulder. "Keep going, sweetheart."

She froze, then licked her lips and slowly drifted to her knees as he unbuckled his belt.

"You use your mouth to put up these walls between us, Mari." He rubbed his thumb over her lower lip, loving how she parted for him and extended her tongue in invitation. He'd give her something to lick in a minute. "That's gotta stop."

"Don't be a buzzkill," she whispered, unzipping his jeans. But her eyes said something much less cheeky. *Trust is hard.*

Sure was. "What do you need to hear, baby?" He stroked her cheek as she reached into his pants and wrapped her cool little hand around his shaft. He closed his eyes for a minute, enjoying her confident tug and twist. How quickly they'd gotten to know each other's bodies. Any second now she'd lick up and around the head of his cock.

He pulled back, replacing her hand with his own. "I think about you all day." He used his other hand to hold her chin, and his thumb to press her lips closed when she started to respond. "Wait. Let that sink in. How much you affect me."

She nipped at his thumb with her teeth. "I know," she said quietly, her eyes firmly gazing up at him. "I'm prickly, but I'm not deluding myself." She licked the full length of his finger. "I think about you all the time, too."

"Just this?" He nudged his cock against her lips and she slowly shook her head back and forth, rubbing all those sensitive nerve endings in exactly the right way. The hot puff of air as she slowly exhaled helped too, and blood pounded in his ears. He was faintly surprised that any remained in his head, sure that it had all flooded to his dick.

"No." She repeated the denial more solemnly this time. "I think about how good it feels to have you around. You're quiet, and considerate. You can cook, which makes me wonder why I've been serving you lunch for the past year." His cock knocked against her mouth, eager to offer an answer, and she laughed.

He took advantage of her parted lips and slide inside. Her eyes flared wide, and he paused, but she swallowed around him and made an appreciative noise that vibrated right through him. He thrust gently, wanting to keep her busy but needing to focus on the right words.

"I'm not going anywhere." His voice had a rough catch to it, but he didn't care. "I'm yours until you tire of me. I promise. Do you hear that?"

She swallowed around him and nodded, her eyes wide and no longer laughing. She was dead serious now, and so was he. He fisted himself and slid out of her mouth, then reached down and hauled her up, not caring at all that his junk was hanging out of his pants.

"I love you," he growled against her lips, then kissed her before she had a chance to say "thank you" or "okay" or "and I really like you a lot", whatever bullshit platitude she'd offer to make him feel like less of a chump.

She didn't need to feel the same way. It wasn't a tit-for-tat exchange. He'd stumbled into this relationship looking to hide a bit longer from reality and, without doing anything other than being herself, she'd cracked open his armoured shell and healed his broken heart. He thought he'd never get over his career ending like that, just when he was hitting his stride. He'd done a bang-up job lying to himself and everyone else. But shit happened, and life went on. He'd said that how many times without meaning it? He was a lucky fuck that karma gave him a pass and still delivered Mari into his life.

And left her there for a solid year while he buried his head in the sand.

He poured his all into this kiss. It would never be enough to properly convey how he felt, but maybe that was a good thing. He'd already probably freaked her out with the l-word.

But she was holding on to him for dear life, and her mouth was as hungry as his. Her hands were under his shirt and in his pants and...oh. Oh. Damn, she wanted him naked. He was processing a bit slowly at the moment. She probably would have asked if he'd given her a chance to come up for air. He broke back, chest heaving, and whipped off his shirt.

She did the same, then leapt at him again. "Chase," she murmured, kissing his jaw and his neck, a million little kisses that each felt like a whisper of something close to three little words.

"Let me show you," he muttered, backing her toward her ridiculously small bedroom. Their jeans fell off in the doorway. He may have ripped off her underwear as they tumbled on top of the blankets. He'd buy her an entire store of underwear to replace it. She'd give him a look that said *that's not necessary* and he'd kiss her until she didn't care anymore.

As he crawled over her, Mari proved she wasn't going to be *shown* anything. She was taking, hungrily, barely giving him a chance to touch and taste before she moved against him. Her hands splayed across his lower abdomen, tracing the ridges there as he held himself over her.

"You're so beautiful," she said, but her attention wasn't on one of his muscles. Her fingertip circled a small white scar, one of a four he had from exploratory surgery after the accident. He grunted as she slid her hand lower, teasing at the edge of his pubic hair before curving around his ass, groping him as she slid her legs between his.

She was equal parts soft skin and firm muscle, and he couldn't get enough. He braced himself on one arm and slid his other hand down to her hip, loving the way her thigh worked under his palm as she ground herself against him.

"Let me make you feel good," he whispered, kissing her temple as he coaxed her to relax on the bed. "Spread your beautiful legs for me, sweetheart. Let me feel how much you want this."

"So much," she moaned, tipping her pelvis up to welcome his fingers. "I want you right there. All of you."

"We've got all night," he crooned, although his erection begged to disagree. *Bury deep*, his cock demanded, and he would in good time. "I want you to come on my fingers first."

"Maybe later," she countered, folding her left leg up and away from her body. The dim, warm yellow light from the lamp bounced across the dips and swells of her long, slim torso, and he was so captivated by the bounce and jiggle of her breasts that he missed her wiggle as she lined up their sexes.

He could never miss the wet welcome of her pussy, though. He nearly sank into her without thinking, just feeling, and it took all of his willpower to jerk his hips back. "Condom," he muttered, and she pointed to a box set out on top of the dresser.

This wasn't how this was supposed to happen. He wanted to tease and caress her, make slow sweet love to her and show her how special she was to him.

But as he turned back to the bed, and found Mari spread eagle with her fingers busy between her legs, all that went out the window.

He needed her. He needed her more than air, and he needed her now.

He rolled on the protection, squeezing his cock at the base for a minute when Mari's gaze lingered there.

And then he was falling between her legs, and into her in more ways than one. She curved her legs high up at his side, arching her back and tipping her hips to seat him as deep as possible inside her impossible warmth.

Tight, wet, warm. The best feeling in the world, and then it got even better as he started thrusting.

— —

Chase loved her. And now he was loving her, hard and fast, and her orgasm was building at a furious pace. She wanted to slow down, feel the delicious layers pile on as he moved inside her, but there was no hope of this freight train putting on any brakes.

She dug her heels into his back and grabbed onto his

shoulders. How many times had she imagined this? And it all felt even better than she'd wanted it to. Above her, he was shaking and surging and while his face was mostly in shadow, he was definitely watching her.

The memory of the night before slammed into her. She got it now. She wanted to see him come too. "Chase," she whispered, then repeated his name louder as she gave herself over to the sensation pounding through her veins.

She locked her eyes on his. "Come with me," she begged. "Chase, please."

He spread his legs wide, pistoning harder into her. "I'm there. Come for me."

"Chase," she screamed, spasming from head to toe. "Oh my god. I love you. You feel so good. Keep doing that forever." She heard herself say it—all of it, but particularly the love part—and suddenly it wasn't so scary. The crazy blissful hormone rush might account for some of that ease, but loving Chase wasn't so hard. It was pretty damn awesome, actually.

He surged above her, eyes watching the whole time like he knew what she was thinking and he was right there with her. He drove hard and deep one last time, then dropped on top of her, burying his face in her neck. She wrapped herself around him, not ready to let go.

# CHAPTER SEVENTEEN

Chase patted her hip. "Need to deal with the condom, baby." She reluctantly let him up, but he came back immediately and lay down next to her. "That was fast. I'm sorry."

She stared at him. "Sorry? That was awesome."

He grinned. "Yeah?"

"Oh, yeah." She didn't miss the glint in his eyes. "Shut up, you knew that."

"Maybe. But I got kind of carried away. You felt amazing." He slowly dragged his hand down her chest. His finger span was so wide he covered most of her torso as he went, leaving a wide trail of electrical sparks in his wake. "Give me fifteen minutes to recuperate and I'm going to show you all the different ways I want to make love to you."

A hot, needy pulse made itself known deep in her pelvis. She bit her lip to keep from grinding against him. "I've got a few different things I want to do to you as well," she admitted.

"Good." He pulled her against him and they lay there for a few minutes as their breathing returned to normal. Chase, naked in her bed, was becoming the most delicious regular occurrence. She was a lucky woman.

When his grip on her relaxed, she rolled over onto her stomach, stretching out. She half-buried her face in her pillow, so only her eyes were peeking out toward him. "Want to talk more now?"

Chase grabbed his chest in mock-shock. "Wait, did Mari Beadie just offer to *talk*?"

She nodded, biting her lip.

He smiled, slow and happy, and smoothed his fingers down her naked spine. He stopped in the small of her back, his hand warm and rough on her skin. She felt wonderful, from the inside out, and *light*. It had been a long day, but she wasn't tired in the least. She wanted to stay up talking all night. He relaxed against his pillow—and how quickly had *that* happened, that he had a side on her bed and everything?—and quietly looked at her.

"What, you want me to go first?" She laughed quietly, then took a slow, settling breath. "I do love you, you know."

"I had some hope. You screamed it mid-orgasm." His eyes twinkled like a man confident in his abilities to please, even when in a hurry. As he should be. He'd pleased her but good.

"I thought maybe I should say it again." But it wasn't just to reassure him. "And I like to say it. A lot."

"Don't let me stop you."

She wiggled her hand up the bed and laced their fingers together next to her head. "I love you, Mr. Grumpy Pants." She wiggled her feet, and Chase reached behind him, grabbed the blanket and arranged it over their lower bodies. "Thank you. So can I ask you about hockey?"

He gave her a surprised look. "Sure."

"You don't mind talking about it?"

"With you? No, not at all." He gave her a long, solemn look. "I might ask for some sharing in return, if you can manage."

She flushed in embarrassment. "I've been really prickly, I'm sorry."

"No need." He shifted to look at her more full-on. "What do you want to know?"

"How old were you when you left home?"

"Sixteen. I went to play for the Peterborough Petes and finished high school there."

"Wow. Did you live on your own?"

"Nah. I had a family I was billeted with. The Carsons.

They were nice. Six kids, all hockey players."

"In the NHL?" He laughed and she frowned. "What, is that funny?"

"Yeah, a little. Sorry. No, they all played amateur hockey through high school, though."

"It's pretty rare, making it to the highest level, then?"

He nodded. "That's something we keep talking about in therapy. That I should stay focused on the success of spending almost a decade in the league."

She counted backwards. "So you didn't go in the NHL right out of school?"

He shook his head. "Some guys do. First draft picks, for example. I wasn't on anyone's radar, though, not seriously, so I stayed in Peterborough for two years after I graduated high school, and I took some courses part-time at the university there."

"Really? Why don't you go back and finish your degree?"

He blushed. "I don't need to."

"Well, sure, but there's something about that accomplishment that's pretty cool."

"I mean, I don't need to because I already did."

"When?"

"Over the summers. I took two courses a year until they mailed me my degree."

"That's amazing. You didn't go to your convocation?"

He made a face. "Not my thing."

"How is it different than skating in front of ten thousand fans in an arena?"

"It just is. Hockey…I've been watched doing that since I was ten, if that makes sense. I literally can't remember a time when I didn't play the game, and it's always been for public consumption. The game. Not me."

"You probably could have gone without it being a spectacle. You come into the bar most days without anyone bugging you now."

He smiled again. "Let it go, sweetheart. All the stages in the world are yours, and that makes me happy. I'll stay at home with a pile of books."

It boggled her mind, but she changed the subject anyway. "So when did you move to Phoenix?"

"After my last year with the Petes, I was invited to the Coyotes training camp for a tryout. Everything worked that week, and they signed me. I spent the next year at their farm team in Utah, then San Antonio for almost two years. Then I was called up."

Mari did the math in her head. "So you played in the NHL for eight years?"

"Nine. Well…" he trailed off and laughed. "There was some back and forth between Phoenix and San Antonio for a while. There's an adjustment period."

"That makes me feel better," she admitted.

"About what?" He shifted closer and pressed a kiss to her shoulder. His beard was less scratchy than the day before, and she lifted her hand to caress his jaw.

"I like your scruff at this length. The hair's curling under, and it's all soft, but still short…" A memory of how his beard felt against the inside of her thighs shuddered through her and she drifted off, suddenly all hot and achey.

"Jesus, Mari, don't look at me like that when we're trying to talk." His voice caught mid-sentence, and she rolled onto her side, baring her breasts to him. "Get back on your tummy, woman, and finish your damn story."

"Come here," she whispered, and he did, stealing her breath with a hot kiss that matched the searing brand between his legs. She shoved him onto his back and climbed on top, desperate to have him fill her again.

With a groaning chuckle, he gave up and reached for a condom, rolling it before lifting her hips, his fingers curving around to the soft flesh of her behind, as she wrapped her fingers around his shaft and guided him home.

— —

"One of these days we're going to actually finish a

conversation," Chase said, throwing his arm over his eyes. Mari blew a cooling breath across his sweat soaked chest.

"In the shower?"

He made an *in a minute* hand gesture, and she bopped out of bed like two rounds of late night sex had invigorated her. Maybe it had. She was so much younger than him. And prettier. And softer.

And just like that, his dick twitched back to life and Chase was off to join his woman. They cleaned up, twice, then fell asleep right after their damp heads hit the pillows again.

The next morning he awoke to the gentle strains of acoustic guitar music. That reminded him that his phone had died when he tried to check out Mari's YouTube page, and he looked around the room for his jeans. He found them crumbled in a pile with Mari's in the doorway. Which meant that she'd stepped over them on the way to play her guitar.

He shook his head with a sigh. Well, he was retired. He could be in charge of picking up laundry.

His phone was still in his back pocket. Still dead. He slid his jeans on, not bothering to do up all the buttons, and folded Mari's and put them on her dresser after making the bed. He scratched the back of his head, wondering where he'd left his shirt. Somewhere between the bedroom and the front door. But he didn't get that far before finding it—on Mari. She glanced up, her smile glowing, and stopped playing.

"Good morning," she said, setting her guitar aside. She walked across the room to him, all bare legs and bouncy hair, and by the time she reached him the blood was pounding in his veins.

"Breakfast first, you insatiable woman," he muttered before taking her mouth in a quick kiss. "And can I plug my phone in?"

She pointed to a cord cleverly fed through a hole in the back of a bookcase. He set his phone to charge and went to the kitchen to make coffee, then checked the fridge. She didn't have enough eggs for omelets, but there was bacon, tomato and bread. Toasted sandwiches it was. He had the first one plated when his phone finally came back to life—and started chiming like something was on fire.

He'd turned off all the social media notifications, so that had to be a hell of a lot of text messages. He quickly plated the second sandwich and carried them both to the table. Mari was already on her way to the kitchen.

"I'll grab our coffees," she said quietly as he grabbed his phone. He couldn't move very far, tethered to the wall like that, so when she gave him a curious look on her return, he waved her over.

The first three had been from his sister Karen, all about a party she wanted to throw for his parents. He deleted all of them. He'd ask her later and she could put whatever she wanted him to do directly in his calendar. But as Mari tucked herself under his arm, he opened the first of nineteen text messages from Audrey. *What the hell?*

**Dude. Have you read The Filthy today?**

**No, of course you haven't.**

**Remind me to say you're welcome for monitoring your Google Alerts for you.**

A cold tendril of unease curled through his gut. Of course he knew what *The Filthy* was—a repugnant gossip blog. Tons of his friends and teammates in the league had been covered by them, but he'd never rated high enough.

**Kelly is a fucking piece of work.**

**Hellooooo? You need to get ahead of this.**

That was as far as he got before his phone rang, but it wasn't Audrey. It was Oscar. Chase's thumb hovered over the "DECLINE" button, but Mari was watching him. He clenched his jaw and stabbed at the screen. "Oscar. To what do I owe this early morning call?"

"Even earlier for me, Chase, I'm in L.A. right now." His friend sighed. "There's a thing you need to see on The Filthy."

"So I hear. My sister sent me a dozen texts about it this

morning. I haven't read them all. Do you want to give me a sneak peek at whatever lies I might be in for?"

"Pissed off ex-girlfriends?"

"I only have one of those."

"The Filthy thinks you've got two, one of them is a reality TV star wannabe, and—Chase, there's more."

Against his side, Mari stiffened. She could clearly hear their conversation. She tried to step away, but Chase tightened his hold on her. Whatever this nonsense was, they'd deal with it together. Or he'd deal with it, quietly and with the best lawyers money could buy, all the while holding her kicking and screaming behind his back. Yeah, that sounded about right.

"They're wrong. Big surprise. Can you email me a link?"

"Already did."

"Thanks, man."

"Don't mention it."

"Listen, how much rage am I in for when I click on that link?"

"It depends on how much you care about this other woman."

Fuck. Mari was staring up at him with Bambi eyes. "A lot."

"You might want to sit down and take some deep breaths first." That didn't help his blood pressure.

He held his phone tight in his fist for a minute before opening his email. Not as many unread messages there, and the most recent one was the link from Oscar. Before he could click on it, though, the phone rang and this time it was his baby sister.

"Audrey, we just woke up—"

"You're at Mari's?"

He took a deep breath. "Yes. Where else would I be?"

"Drinking in a pathetic dive bar?"

"Well, I'm not."

She paused, clearly waiting for more information, but he didn't have any. "Did you get my text messages?"

"I've read maybe a third of them. I was on the phone with Oscar."

"So Mari doesn't hate you?"

"Not that I know of."

"But you stayed over last night."

"Not really any of your business, Aud."

"No, that's good. That's really good. I'll let you go. Just keep her happy."

Now he was annoyed *and* confused. Great.

He hung up the phone and instead of going back to Oscar's email, he put it on the shelf. He needed a hug, and something told him he needed to hold on to Mari.

"Come on." He steered her to the couch, dropping heavily into the middle of it and pulling her into his lap.

"What the hell is going on?" She burrowed tight against him as he told her what he knew, which wasn't much.

"Do you want to look at it together or on your own?"

His grip tightened around her waist. "Together."

— —

Mari couldn't breathe properly. "I didn't...I haven't posted anything about you online," she whispered. Chase held her tightly, but she was afraid he'd stop when he saw her name on a story dragging him back into the limelight in an ugly way. Afraid she'd taken some accidental misstep that would tear apart the best thing she'd ever had, all because it was new and fragile. Not nearly as entrenched as Chase's preference for privacy.

"Never for a second would I think you did, baby." His voice scratched against her heart, gruff and strong. "How many songs have you posted on YouTube?"

Mari closed her eyes and thought about her channel. "Two in the last little while. There are some older live performances as well."

"I didn't watch the one you told me about yesterday because my phone died. Any chance one of the lyrics is

*Chase Miller sucks?"*

She shook her head. No, "Gruff Boy" wouldn't be the problem. Before they even looked at the story, she knew if they'd latched on to any of her songs it would be "Special." She took a deep breath. "There's another song. It's not about you." It had been, for a minute, but by the time she'd finished it, she knew that wasn't Chase. "But that's it. Just a song. People write songs about all sorts of things."

He sighed, and she didn't know how to read that. "Okay. Can we look at it on your computer?"

She nodded numbly and grabbed her laptop off the coffee table. She handed it over, then curled up against his side. He opened a browser and Google searched for the blog. The first post was about a drunk heiress who'd lost her underwear, and included pictures. Chase quickly scrolled down, almost zooming past his picture. A picture of him and Kelly, actually. It was taken at night, coming out of a restaurant.

"That's old," he muttered under his breath, and she thought it was to himself until he looked over and rubbed her knee. He was reassuring *her*. Damn it, she should be doing that for *him*.

"It's okay," she whispered.

The headline was crude. **The Incomprehensible Sex Appeal of the Has-Been Hockey Player: Coyote Chase Miller's Trail of Rejects**.

"I wouldn't have thought any Filthy bloggers would know the word incomprehensible," Chase said, derision dripping from every word. He clicked on the link, but before the story could even load, he closed the laptop.

They sat there for a minute, Mari watching Chase and Chase staring straight ahead at the wall. Then he cursed under his breath and opened the computer again. She squeezed his arm, feeling totally out of her depth and unsure of what words might help—if any could.

The story was short, crazy and painful to read. But it was also backed up with pictures. Mari hadn't even finished reading before Chase shoved off the couch, set the laptop on the coffee table, and stalked back to his phone.

Left alone with the computer, Mari started again at the beginning. Claims of alcoholism, flights back and forth to Phoenix, a reckless affair with a local bartender who was an aspiring songwriter willing to do anything for a little publicity, and regular visits to his loft *at his parents' home* by a high-price call girl. There was no mistaking the Miller home in the background.

Before, she'd just been struggling to get enough air to think clearly. Now Mari stopped breathing, full stop.

"Don't read that shit," he growled from behind her, and she dropped her face into her hands. This wasn't about her songs. This was way worse. She was nothing but a line, a filler bit of fluff in a gossip piece.

A deep, wide ocean of experience and status separated them. She was a little girl with big dreams, and Chase was a man done with that world. But that world wasn't done with him—and it wasn't interested in her. Which was good right now. She wasn't the cause of Chase's pain. But it also underlined how selfish she was, that she even thought about that at a time like this.

Behind her, Chase started talking rapidly into the phone. "It's urgent I speak with Dr. Mettner. No, you don't understand, this isn't a patient request. No, I am a patient, but I'm also—hey, there's no need to be rude. I know you have a secret emergency code that you can send her. Do that now. Tell her Chase Miller needs to speak to her this morning, preferably before she goes anywhere in public. It's for her own—no, I'm not threatening her. Oh for God's sake."

He slammed the phone back down on the shelf, and she turned around in time to see him glare at it and stalk back toward the couch. He leaned over the back of it, grabbing her forearms, and pulled her up to stand, wrapping his arms around her waist. "Baby, it's not true. Any of it."

"Is Dr. Mettner a hooker?" she whispered, knowing that

didn't quite make sense, but she was this close to passing out and complicated thoughts weren't happening.

"Jesus, no. She's my psychologist. And she started coming to see me at my house when I had trouble moving around, and then continued because I pay her extra for the trip. She's a medical professional, Mari. I've never slept with her. Never wanted to."

She nodded dumbly. Right. Yes, of course he hadn't. She knew that.

"The only trip to Phoenix I've taken in the last year was with you."

"I know that, too." She closed her eyes. He kept going, breaking down the lies one by one, but she didn't need to hear it. "Stop, honey. I trust you."

He pulled her tighter around him, his arms bands of protective steel around her waist and up her back. He rubbed his face in her hair before easing back enough to search her face for reassurance. Then he nodded, his lips set firmly in a line. "Come on, let's eat our sandwiches."

"I'm not hungry." God, she sounded petulant. She huffed out a breath. "Okay. Food."

"That's better." He let go of her long enough for her to climb off the couch, then he laced their fingers together. They quietly sat at the table and stared at their breakfast, Chase looking just as shell-shocked as she felt. But he also looked like he knew how to deal with this, which gave him a distinct advantage over her. He squeezed her hand. "I'll call my lawyer while you're at work today. Unless you want to call in?"

She shook her head. Working would be good. Busy. Maybe give her some time to think.

"I'll get that piece of shit story taken down."

She nodded.

He frowned. "Are you okay?"

"Yeah," she breathed, because technically she *was* fine. Nothing had happened to her. "Of course. I should be asking you that question."

His frown deepened, but he didn't say anything. He stared at her until she picked up her sandwich just to have something other than unspoken words in her mouth.

Someone had come to Wardham and taken pictures of her and Chase. Watched her at the bar. Gone to his house and taken pictures of his therapist. Home was no longer a safe haven for him. The realization made her want to cry or throw up or both. She took a big sip of coffee and blinked back tears.

Chase said her name quietly, then repeated it. She just stared at her sandwich and kept chewing. She needed to get through breakfast, then get dressed, then go to work. One foot in front of the other. "Baby," he whispered, and she realized he gotten off his chair and was kneeling at her side. "It's okay to be upset. Someone violated your privacy."

"*Your* privacy. Not mine."

"No," he ground out. "Ours. Mine. Yours. Both of us."

She shook her head, and when that wasn't enough, she closed her eyes. She'd go back to bed if it didn't smell like him. "You should go," she whispered. "In case it looks bad, you being here."

"What the hell? No. I'm not going anywhere." He wrapped his arms around her and picked her up. She wanted to protest but she couldn't. Being in his arms felt too good. He carried her to her bed and curled in next to her. "This is going to go away. It's nothing."

It didn't feel like nothing. "Paparazzi took our pictures."

"Maybe. More likely it was someone local who wanted to make a quick buck. I'm not that famous. There aren't that many bucks to be made off of my imaginary sex life. This is what lawyers are for. I'll handle it." He was saying all the right things. So why was she having a complete meltdown? She buried her face in his chest, letting the warmth of his hand on her back and the comforting depth in his voice sooth her rubbed-raw soul.

Maybe it would be okay. Maybe this was the beginning and the end of it.

# CHAPTER EIGHTEEN

It wasn't going away. By the time he walked Mari over to Danny's for her shift, his lawyer had already drafted a cease and desist letter, and he'd promised Mari a dozen times in a dozen different ways that he'd fix it. Preferably with a nuclear legal bomb, but he wasn't opposed to looking into dirty pool options either.

But when he arrived back at his parents' place, Audrey had the dining room set up like a digital war room. And the self-appointed general was displeased with her intel.

"Who did you piss off?" Audrey demanded when he strode in.

"Fuck if I know. Kelly, I guess, but this doesn't feel like her style. If she wants to snare another professional athlete, she won't want something like this tied to her name."

"There's some private Facebook group chatter about Mari." She winced at his expression, and he could only imagine it was murderous. That's how he felt.

"She's not taking this well. You can't tell her shit like that."

"Well no kidding, she was made to look like one of your harem." Audrey couldn't know how her choice of words impacted him—he had a pretty good poker face—but fuck, wasn't that Mari's fear? She'd joked about it the night before, but early on she'd really thought he was a player.

"This needs to go away."

His sister winced. "It's the internet. You can't vacuum up all the little pieces. I think you need to hire a publicist to reframe the story."

He didn't like where this was going. His idea of the perfect solution was hiring a black hat hacker to lace The Filthy's servers with malware and viruses.

"You haven't given any interviews since the car accident."

"I'm not someone of interest," he exploded. "I'm a washed-up third-liner. No one cares about how I'm doing now."

"Clearly you're wrong. And if you stay silent, then this is your legacy. When it could be something totally different." Audrey spun her laptop toward him and pointed to the screen, and an article in a national magazine that he'd read at the beginning of the summer about Josh Calloway, a guy who's career path was quite similar to his.

"Point taken." His skin crawled at the idea of sitting down with a reporter, but he'd do anything to set the record straight about his relationship with Mari.

"Right now this is a tempest in a teapot. Let's keep it that way." Audrey's phone beeped and she tapped furiously at the screen.

"You scare me, you know that?"

"Excellent. Now let's fix this before I leave next week, okay? I'll worry about you while I'm gone if we don't."

He nodded and stepped back outside to call Oscar. Sitting on the porch and looking at the lake while torturing himself would be a good balance. But he wouldn't be alone. His dad sat on the wicker settee, nursing a beer.

Chase sighed. "Where did you magically appear from?"

"Just got home. Audrey sent me a 911 text."

"She's a force of nature, eh?" Chase nodded to the beer. "You got another one of those of me?"

His dad leaned over to the bar fridge tucked into the corner and handed over a bottle. Then he pinned Chase down with a heavy glare. "You weren't a third-liner."

"Not always, no." Chase rolled his shoulders and looked down at his feet.

"You did it the hard way, and you did it well. You really

hit your stride the last two years."

"Dad, I know…"

"You clearly don't, Chad. I heard what your sister said, and she's smart as a whip, but you've gotta get your story sorted out. Not made up. The truth, the best way it shows you."

"I don't care, Dad. That's the thing. I'm never going to be in a history book."

"I didn't realize that was important to you."

"It's not." *Shit. Shit, shit, shit, shit, shit.* Maybe it was a little. Chase's heart rate picked up, his pulse thumping in his ears. His dad lifted his brow and tipped back his beer. Chase sighed.

"You might not care about being famous, son, and I can respect that. But we all want to have a proud legacy."

"Why?" He shook his head. "I swear, I've never cared before."

His dad let out a wry laugh. "You've never been in love before, either. First comes marriage, then comes babies. And I'm telling you, there's nothing more motivating than being a hero to your children."

Damnit, his eyes were *not* vaguely wet at that idea. Not at all. His dad laughed and handed over another beer, but Chase waved it off. "Nah. I've got a couple of calls to make."

"I'll leave you to that, then." Hank stood and clapped his hand on Chase's shoulder. "One day, your son will win the Stanley Cup. Or the Nobel Prize. Or something equally amazing and far beyond anything you did. And that will be your legacy. Your life's work isn't over. It's just beginning."

Jesus. His dad needed to stop being profound before Chase embarrassed them both. "Got it, Dad."

"Because—"

"Seriously. Point taken. Now I gotta find a way to prove to my girl that I can be all that and a bag of chips, so you want to leave me to it?"

His dad chuckled and wished him luck.

— —

Audrey and Stella came in to Danny's at the dinner lull—they did a decent lunch service, but no one in Wardham wanted a sandwich for their evening meal. Farmers had chores, people in town had after school activities with their kids. Things would pick up again in the evening, but for now she wasn't busy. Which was a shame, because the last thing she wanted was to talk.

"Out," Mari said, pointing to the door. "I'm playing the happy bartender here, no room for worried friends."

"Who says we aren't here to gawk at Wardham's newest celebrity?" Stella said, perching herself on a stool.

Mari blew a raspberry. "That's not me. The only photos they used of me were blurry. And I haven't had many clicks on my YouTube video, either. I'm a nobody in this story."

Audrey frowned and sat down too. "You say that like it's a bad thing."

"No. No!" Mari shook her head vigorously. "Not at all. The last thing I want is random notoriety. But I keep waiting for the other shoe to drop. For a pile of paparazzi to pile in through the door or something."

Audrey opened her mouth to say something else, but Stella grabbed her arm and changed the subject. "Can we have a drink, happy bartender?"

Mari gave her best friend a relieved smile—Stella held that title for a reason. "Sure, what do you want?"

"Beer's good."

Mari poured them lager half-pints, then leaned on the bar between them. She looked at Audrey first. "I'm not handling this well, but I promise I'm never going to want to profit from your brother's fame."

Audrey squeezed her hand. "I know, sweetie. But it might be a bit late for that."

"What do you mean?"

The other woman pressed her lips together and Mari

swivelled to Stella. "What's she talking about?"

Stella shook her head. "Not my circus, not my monkeys."

"Excuse me?"

"It's a Polish proverb. It means this isn't my crazy to get involved in, so I'm going to sit here and drink this beer."

Mari turned back to Audrey, who was taking the world's longest, slowest sip of beer. She shrugged and pointed to the glass pressed against her mouth. Mari crossed her arms and waited.

Finally Audrey set her glass down with a sigh. "I may have suggested that he put his own story out there. On a different site. Not a response, exactly. Just different noise to fill up the Google search on Chase Miller."

Mari slowly nodded. "That's actually really smart."

Audrey bit her lip. "Well, Chase's story of the last year of his life…it's the story of you."

Something heavy slid down the back of Mari's neck and wrapped itself around her chest. Something warm and dark and lovely and scary. "What?" she breathed.

"So it's a little late to not make this about you, because he's done that. Kind of in a big way."

Little white spots appeared in the corners of her field of vision.

Stella leaned forward over the bar. "Take a deep breath."

She couldn't. "Define big way," she squeaked.

"Have you heard of Reddit?" Mari nodded, so Audrey continued. "It started with an *Ask Me Anything* post there this afternoon. That's still going on. He handled the hecklers like a boss, and once the mods knew he was legitimately who he said he was, they started helping too."

Her fingers itched to reach for her phone, but she gripped them in front of her instead. "What else?"

"A couple of call-ins to sports talk radio in Detroit, and tomorrow he's doing a live podcast with the guys on *The Stick*." Mari must have given her a blank look, because Audrey hastened to explain it was a popular hockey blog.

"It's being hyped pretty hard on the hockey forums."

"Okay…" None of that sounded like a big deal. Hockey fans would be more interested in Chase than her.

"And Oscar got him a publicist who's currently working on getting the two of you a feature article in one of the big news magazines."

Oh. "Where is he now?"

"He'll be here soon, I think. He was on the phone when I left."

Mari pointed her finger at her friend. "You came here to see how I reacted when he showed up!"

"Well, yeah. It's super romantic. It'll be like a live-action, twenty-first-century version of *The Notebook*."

Stella twisted her head to the side. "You've never seen *The Notebook*, have you?"

Audrey shook her head. "No. Is it good?"

Stella sighed as Audrey cackled beside her. "You're missing out." She looked back at Mari. "But she's right, it's totally romantic and I want a front row seat for the *Dirty Dancing* leap you're going to take into his arms."

Mari slowly got turned and grabbed the Patron off the wall. She needed a shot for courage.

Stella stared at her. "What's wrong? Why do you look so freaked out?"

She couldn't explain how terrifying it was that Chase had no qualms about being a permanent couple—linking his name to her in every possible medium. After a few weeks and a handful of dates, most of those under the pretence of pretending to date.

She tossed back another shot. "That's not the relationship we have," she whispered. "We agreed. No romance."

"Sometimes things change," Audrey said, uncharacteristically quiet. "You aren't mad at him, are you?"

She shook her head. "God, no. Just…overwhelmed. I don't come from a demonstrative family—I'm not even sure if my parents love each other." Now she was babbling, but she couldn't stop. "I mean, I know they *love* each other, but it's quiet. And I thought that if I ever fell in love, that's what it would be like. Safe. Quiet." *Reliable*, she added in her head. But Chase was that, wasn't he? He wasn't going anywhere. He'd gone to great lengths to make that clear. And when shit hit the fan, he carried all the burden on his wide shoulders.

"But your parents have such a romantic story," Stella protested.

Mari shook her head. They loved each other, and she knew her dad loved his kids as much as he would if they were biologically his, but they'd come together in a very business-like manner. Her mother had a farm that needed a farmer. Mark had had all the skills and no land—and had probably been a thirty-year-old virgin, although she didn't want to think too much about that. He was definitely a shy man, morally conservative. Nothing like her birth father, who'd been charismatic and totally into her mother right up until it all got a bit too hard.

Passion didn't last forever. Passion got you knocked up three times over, then abandoned.

Except that didn't seem true for her friends. She thought of Carrie and Ian, and Karen and Paul. They had passion and commitment in spades.

She just never thought it would happen to *her*.

And now that it had…was she ready for it?

— —

Chase was beyond nervous as he parked in front of Danny's.

He'd acted on a huge assumption today, that Mari was in fact his. He'd probably overstated their relationship in a dozen different ways, but the thought of anyone thinking otherwise made his blood boil.

But now, looking at the pub, he was reminded he had no claim beside the blinding love he felt for her. But while it was a new experience, he'd never been more sure of himself. And never more scared—because he could make all the grand gestures in the world and they'd only work if Mari's love were equally sure.

He stepped inside, not surprised in the least to see his sister sitting at the bar. She'd disappeared when he was on the phone and for once he didn't mind. Maybe she'd softened Mari up a bit.

The object of his affection was drying a glass that looked pretty shiny and dry already. She gave him an inscrutable look.

"Hey." Not the strongest of openers.

She gave him a stern double blink in response.

"So I managed to bury that story on the third page of a Google search."

A harsh, watery laugh burst out of her. "Yeah? How'd you do that?"

"It turns out that people like to know about professional athletes' private lives—the good, censored kind of sharing, don't worry."

"I wouldn't say I'm worried, exactly."

"What are you?"

"Overwhelmed?"

"Yeah. But I took care of it."

"Without telling me anything!"

Shit. That sounded like something he should have anticipated. "I told you I'd take care of it."

"And boy howdy you did, eh?" She put down the glass and tipped her head to the end of the bar. It wasn't exactly a private conversation spot, but it would do.

"Hey, did I mess up?" He asked gruffly as she wrapped her arms around his waist once they no longer had the bar separating them. Now they had a giant miscommunication settling there instead.

"I have no idea, because I haven't read your answers to the Reddit AMA," she muttered under her breath.

He'd thought that would have been good, shielding her

from the crap people threw online. He'd been wrong. He'd thought he'd seen through her tough exterior and discovered she was soft and needy. He'd liked that, that he could be the tough guy, the alpha male to save her when she was weak. Turns out the joke was on him. At her core, Mari was pure steel, and she didn't have time for any shit.

Which shouldn't be a surprise, she'd told him that all along. He'd just chosen not to hear it.

"I only said good things about you," he said into her hair. She felt small but tough in his arms, like a fighter, and he realized that he'd missed that this morning—she'd been shocked, but when had Mari ever backed down from a challenge? "And it's still going on. You can pop in and take me to town if you want."

She laughed and sighed into his chest. "No. But it's all so...I mean, an article about us? I don't even know what we are yet."

He froze. "I didn't think there was any doubt on that question. Was I wrong?"

She pushed away from him. She didn't go far, and didn't push hard, but there was a wary look in her eye that he didn't understand—or like. Fight or flight...it wasn't even a question. He'd fight for her, forever, but he didn't think that the battle would be *between* them.

"I know we were supposed to have more time." He took a deep breath. "A few days ago I wasn't sure if you were going to let me *kiss* you again. And then this morning all hell broke lose and all I could think about was protecting you. Changing the narrative before it could even touch you."

He stopped to think for a second, but she'd obviously heard enough. "No, stop. It's okay."

It didn't sound okay. "There's more." He raked his hands through his hair. He needed a minute to collect his thoughts. To get it *right*.

"Maybe we've had enough for one day."

He frowned. "What are you saying?"

She shook her head. "I'm not saying anything other than

I want a hot shower and a soft pillow. I want to go to bed and not think about this again until tomorrow."

He closed his eyes. "Okay. If that's what you want."

She stepped closer, pressing herself against him. "Please don't think I'm not grateful. I get to pretend none of this is happening because I know you're taking care of it."

He grunted. That was small comfort if she still needed distance.

She wrapped her arms around him and sighed, rubbing her face against his chest for a minute. Then she groaned and stepped back. "Okay."

He nodded and watched her head for the door, his heart cracking apart. It wasn't goodbye, it wasn't even a break or a break-up, but damnit, he needed her tonight. Every night, but especially tonight.

She stopped and turned back. "Chase?"

"Yeah?" His voice rasped and he didn't care. He also didn't care that they weren't alone in the bar. His sister was staring at them with rapt attention, and at some point Stella had slid behind the bar, taking Mari's place.

Mari blinked at him and held out her hand. "Aren't you coming?"

# CHAPTER NINETEEN

"Stop touching the blindfold." Mari twisted toward the sound of Chase's voice, all warm and amused.

"It's kind of itchy."

"It's a five-hundred-dollar tie."

"That's a stupid amount of money to spend on a tie, particularly one that is itchy for the women you tie up."

"Keep up the snark, baby, and I'm going to use the other pieces of over-priced silk I own to strap you to your bedposts when we get back."

That actually sounded kind of awesome, but this surprise was making Chase happy, so she bit her lip and stayed quiet as his truck slowed down and made a turn.

It had been a hellish week. Not because of the Internet, although she regretted setting up a Google Alert. Chase had just looked at her balefully and shook his head. Well, she couldn't not keep track of it all once she knew it was out there.

But the rumours never made it to the mainstream media, just swirled for a day or two on the scuzzier gossip blogs. Chase's whirlwind media blitz had worked, and taken on a life of its own as he opened up about depression and professional athletes post-retirement. But it had meant two days of flying back and forth to Toronto and New York City, and one long day of interviews and photographs at the Miller home and at her apartment.

*Her apartment.* That hadn't freaked her out or anything. But Chase's message had been simple: there was more to life than a career, and he'd discovered that lovely truth in his girlfriend's Goodwill-chic apartment. Where she wrote songs. *Good songs*, he kept telling people. And her YouTube counter kept climbing.

And then this morning they'd been emailed an advance look at next week's cover of *Maclean's*, the national newsmagazine. Mari on her couch, playing the guitar, with Chase doing sit-ups at her feet.

It was ridiculous. Totally over the top. And she secretly wanted a poster-sized print of it.

They hadn't talked as much as they probably should have this week. After that night in the bar, they'd gone back to her place and showered together, then made the slow, sweet kind of love that said more than words ever could.

But now they finally had a day for the two of them, and Chase had this big plan...when really, they should have stayed in bed—PJs on—and talked about it all.

The truck came to a stop, and she brought her hands up to her face, but he was faster than her. His callous-roughened hands slid over hers, holding her still. "What's on your mind?"

She shook her head. "Nothing."

He laughed, low and warm, and his breath puffed across her face. He kissed her cheek as he unbuckled her seat belt, then his thigh slid against hers. He was crowding her, and she wanted him even closer. "You've always got something on your mind, baby. Are you thinking about a song? Or is it us?"

"You're far too observant for your own good," she grumbled. "I was just thinking that we haven't talked a lot this week."

He nodded, his stubbled cheek shifting against hers. "It's been a go-go-go kind of week. What do you want to talk about?"

Nothing. Everything. "I love you," she started. He needed to know that. It trumped everything else. "But I'm scared, I guess."

"Are you still overwhelmed?"

She let out a helpless little laugh and burrowed closer. "Still...maybe always will be."

He reached between them and slid the blindfold onto her forehead. She blinked at him. God, his face made her so happy. She stroked his cheek and he twisted his face, pressing a kiss into the palm of her hand.

"I want the world for you, Mari," he said solemnly. "I don't want to stand in your way. I want to pave it. Move mountains to make your dreams a reality. You need studio time? I'll fly you to New York. I'll build you a studio so you can record songs overlooking the lake. Or I'll drive you back and forth to Detroit and do Starbucks runs as often as you want. Whatever you want, it's yours. Whatever you need, I'll make it happen. Because you've already done that for me."

"You keep saying that," she whispered. "But I didn't do anything." A soft buzzing sound filled her ears. What had she done to deserve this love? What if he was mistaken, and when he realized how one-sided their relationship was, he'd resent her?

"No frowning, sweetheart." Chase cupped her face and smoothed his thumb over her cheekbone. "I think this is supposed to be one of those happy moments in a relationship. We're talking about how special we are to each other." He narrowed his eyes. "I am special to you, right?"

"That's exactly it," she sniffed, fighting a losing battle against a flood of desperate tears despite his joke. "I'm not—" she hiccuped. "The thing is, you deserve —"

"You. I deserve you. You make me healthy sandwiches and leave me alone when I'm in a mood. You've got my back, no matter what, and you look at me like the best of me is still to come."

"Of course it is," she whispered.

"The best years of my life are behind me, officially. That's all anyone else sees. They all think it's okay if I retire and spend the rest of my days reading Reddit on my phone and drinking beer in your bar."

"I thought it was Angry Birds, NHL style."

He laughed, and she joined him. "Seriously?"

"Well, not anymore. You have depth, I've learned."

"Nothing wrong with Angry Birds, baby. But seriously, no one else sees me the way you do."

"That's because you don't show them."

"I don't want to. I only want to show you."

"Why?"

He stared at her for a long, lingering, smoking hot minute. "Because you're my better half. You made me whole. Without you I was just a broken man, leading a broken life. And then you shoved your sunshine down my throat and damned if you didn't heal me from the inside out."

"I don't feel like sunshine right now. I feel all fragile."

He pulled back. "Come on."

She blinked and looked past him. They were at an apple orchard not far from town.

"I'm game for talking as much as you want, baby, but I think we deserve a little bit of normal in our life today. Like a date to go apple picking."

She laughed. "You just want to press me up against a tree and make out."

"Maybe. Come on."

He tugged her out his door, catching her around her waist as she jumped off the running board. He held her gaze for a minute, making her tummy do awesome flip-floppy things, then grabbed a bushel basket from the back.

They walked hand-in-hand down the grassy path between the rows of gnarled dwarf apple trees. Chase reached way up high as they passed under an overhanging branch, grabbing a shiny red Jonamac apple. He held it out in offer, and she took a bite and groaned.

"Oh, that's amazing," she whispered, juice spilling over her lips. He grinned and ducked his head, sucking that patch of skin next to her mouth between his lips.

"I agree," he said huskily. His eyes twinkled as he pulled back.

They stopped halfway down the row and started filling the basket. Mari looked for the apples that looked ready to be picked, all over the tree, but Chase stuck to the top branches.

"Do you have something against the apples down here?" she asked, nudging him with her elbow.

"Not at all. But you've got those, so I'll get these." He found another perfect one.

"Yeah, but the ones you pick do look better than mine."

"I'm looking for the ones that have grown in the sun," he said quietly. He glanced down at her, almost shyly. "Like me."

She pressed her lips together at the unexpected well of emotion. "There you go again with those crazy sweet lines."

He took the apple from her hand and set it in the basket, then dropped to the grass and pulled her down, settling her between his legs. He nuzzled her cheek for a moment before kissing his way down her neck. "Some things take longer to mature. Need a little more tender loving care."

"Like late harvest apples," she teased.

"And defencemen," he countered in all seriousness. "I watched guys I played against in the OHL head up to the AHL and even the NHL while I stayed behind. And then it took me a couple more years to iron out the kinks. Hell, I was just hitting my stride when it all ended. I resented that for a while. Now I get that's not just hockey. It's my life. And the best was still to come. I didn't get that until you landed in my lap."

"It's true for me, too, you know." She twisted her fingers into his shirt, wanting to feel his warmth radiate into her skin. He was her sunshine as much as she was his.

"A wary woman?" He pressed a gentle kiss to her lips, and she took a deep, restorative breath.

"More like a little girl who was abandoned before she was even born," she admitted, her voice still shakier than she'd like.

"Jesus," he bit out, wrapping her in his arms. "I'm never

going to do that to you, baby. Never."

He looked so fierce, so protective. She'd never loved him as much as she did in that moment. "Come here," she whispered.

"I think that's my line," he said, laughing, then he covered her mouth with his and the laughter faded into urgency and need. This was more than a kiss, it was a confirmation and a commitment and all that was still left to be said.

They'd get to the words, some day. Probably soon. She loved that he liked to talk. But talking could rub her raw, too, and she loved even more that he got that. Apple picking. The man was a genius in more ways than one.

He rolled them slowly to their sides, nudging a few fallen apples out of the way. He kissed her slowly, thoroughly, and with erotic precision. She rocked against him, wanting more.

"Let's go home," she gasped, sliding her hand under his shirt. His skin was warm and taut there, and she teased her fingertips down the front of his jeans just enough to make sure he knew she was serious about getting some—here or there, she really didn't care at the moment.

He hauled them both up, then kissed her again as he picked grass and leaves out of her hair before picking up the basket of apples and setting back for the truck at double time.

# EPILOGUE

Nothing said Merry Christmas quite like a wake-up blow job.

Chase spread his legs wide and lifted his hips toward the welcoming mouth of his soon-to-be fiancée. So hot and wet. *Jesus.* He laced his hands into her hair, holding her still for a moment, thinking that if he could unscramble his brain cells, maybe this could become something more mutually satisfying. But then her tongue swirled around him and he gave up.

"I'm going to miss this apartment," he gasped when she triumphantly crawled up his chest a few minutes later. "It holds some of my favourite memories."

"What do you want for Christmas breakfast?" she asked, pressing little kisses all over his chest.

"You, in a minute." He closed his eyes and took a deep breath.

"This time next year your house will be built," she murmured. "Will you want to have your whole family over there for the holidays?"

"Our house," he growled. They'd been playing this verbal tug-of-war for a few weeks now, since he'd inked the deal with the architect and the general contractor. "And that's up to you."

"Then let's leave it with our mothers for now. And maybe Karen will want to host something. I just want the morning with you." She pressed her cheek against his chest.

"This is your favourite party of the holidays?"

She nodded and did an exaggerated cat stretch on top of

him that did dangerous things to his blood pressure.

"Mine too," he muttered, sliding his hands down to her hips. He meant to pull her higher and spread her legs on either side of his face, but she rolled away.

"Need coffee. And I have a present I want to give you, too." He watched as she swung her naked self out of bed, then snagged his dress shirt off the floor. That was a pretty picture.

He grabbed his phone. "Turn around, baby."

She did, just barely holding the shirt closed, and he snapped a quick shot. She wagged her finger at him, and he took another. "Chase," she warned, but her voice was warm and her eyes were dark.

"Want to open that shirt for me, baby?" He smirked as she ducked her head and did up a few buttons. She knew he wouldn't take any pictures that compromised her. But sexy as hell shots of her legs peeking out from the bottom of his shirt? Those were fair game.

He took a series of pictures as she laughingly ran out of the room. By the time she came back, carrying two mugs of coffee in one hand and a wrapped box in the other, he'd made the bed, put on pajama pants because proposing naked seemed like a bad idea, and had the ring looped over the tip of his pinky finger.

"Here you go," she said, carefully transferring one of the mugs to his hand that wasn't fisted against his side. He took a sip and set it on the dresser. She crawled onto the bed and knelt in the middle. Sunlight streamed all around her, belying just how cold it was outside. She took a deep breath and held out the gift.

He sat, feeling like a giant next her—even sitting up on her heels, they were the same sitting height. And it was difficult to open the paper and keep the sparkling rock on his finger hidden at all times. But it was worth it when he opened the cardboard box and lifted out a snorkelling mask. Pressed inside the mask, peeking out at him, was a collage of beach and ocean images. And tucked behind the mask was a printout receipt for flights and a reservation at a resort in the Turks and Caicos Islands. The departure date was just two weeks away.

"Since someone paid for my studio fees," she said, smiling with well-deserved pride. "I had some extra money on hand. And I know you've missed swimming…"

This woman amazed him. He shook his head slowly, his own grin spreading just as wide as hers. "I can't wait."

She poked him in the chest. "You're very sneaky, you know. I thought it would be easy to ask your mother to nip into your loft and find your passport."

He laughed. She wouldn't have found it. Like everything else important to him, it was here in Mari's apartment. He'd stashed his fireproof box of documents in her closet more than a month earlier. "You found it, then?"

"When did you move in? I don't remember talking about that." She narrowed her eyes, but readily parted her lips for his kiss.

He pulled back a minute later with a hiss. "Don't distract me. I need to give you your present. Well, the first one. There are more. At the loft. With most of my clothes, by the way. The only thing that's moved in all the way is my heart."

"Awwww." She kissed him again.

"You like that? It's not too cheesy?"

She shook her head. "Christmas morning is a snark-free zone. You can be as cheesy as you want, and I'll eat it up."

Excellent. That worked for him, because there was a lot of soul-baring he wanted to do in a minute. He pushed up to a stand, and she moved the gift box out of the way expectantly. He just stared at her, perched on her knees on the bed, wearing nothing but his shirt. He was the luckiest man in the world.

He cleared his throat and said as much, and when she laughed, he reached for her hand. She took it and he helped her climb off to join in. Then he slowly dropped to one knee in the narrow strip of bare floor in their tiny-ass bedroom that he loved.

"I love this room," he started as she grinned at him. Tears weren't her style, not for this. "It's where we first made love." She pinked up at that, which was hilarious given how she woke him up. "It's where we make up, when we fight."

"We don't fight that often," she whispered, her eyes dancing.

"We should, though. I like making up." He cleared his throat. "I love you, Mari. So damn much. So I thought about all the crazy places I could ask you to be my wife, and it didn't take me long to realize it needed to be here. I don't need a fancy suit or a candlelight dinner, although I think those would have been fitting too, because it's possible that I fell in love with you that weekend in Arizona."

"You look pretty good in a suit." She reached out to touch his face. "I liked that we got dressed up last night."

He'd almost done it then, after the Christmas Eve dinner at her parents' farm. He was glad he'd waited. "You look better in my shirt than I do. And I want you to wear it forever."

She giggled, and he thought about what he'd just said.

"I mean…okay, let me start again." He tipped his head forward and she threaded her fingers through his hair as he nuzzled at her middle. He took a deep breath, then looked up at her again. "I want to be your husband, Mari. I want to stand in front of everyone we know and pledge to love you forever and ever. Then I want to set out to do just that, every day for the rest of my life. I want to make a home with you, a beautiful home that will be waiting for you when you come back from a tour, and that one day we can fill with children who are equally gifted in music and sport. I want to make you laugh and hold you when you cry, and make love to you as often as possible until we're wrinkled and grey."

"And then?" She had his face in both of her hands now, and she was still grinning, but her eyes were bright and shiny.

"And then we'll get hip replacement surgeries and keep

going at it like bunnies." He took a deep breath and flipped the ring from his pinky to between his thumb and index finger. He'd practiced that move for an hour the week before. Old habits and all that. "Will you make me the happiest man in the entire world and marry me?"

She was nodding before he even finished the question. He stood and twisted them both to fall on the bed in a tumble of limbs and grins and kisses. She slid the ring onto her left hand and waved it in the air. "Wow," she said, laughing. "It's sparkly."

"Like you."

She tossed her arms around his neck and kissed him soundly. He took the opportunity to palm her naked butt, which made her shiver and spread her legs. He slowed down, kissing her more languidly as he stripped their clothes away.

He rose between her legs and stared down at his future wife. "Merry Christmas, baby."

## THE END

# ACKNOWLEDGMENTS
## aka The People Who Keep Me Going

Other than being a proud London Knights fan, my hockey knowledge is woefully limited. So right off the top, I need to thank Melanie Ting and Kate Willoughby for patiently (and temporarily) including me in their ranks as a hockey romance author. Now that Chase is officially retired, I can return to my more comfortable post as a hockey romance reader. Any tidbits I got right can probably be credited to them. Any errors are because I was too busy pinning hot guys to my Pinterest board while they tried to help me. They're both wonderful. Go read their books.

Elle Rush and Amity Lassiter are the other two writing sprint friends I mentioned in the dedication. Their encouragement and appreciation of Chase's pursuit of Mari was equally valuable support!

Anne Marsh, critique partner extraordinaire. You make me laugh out loud while pointing out all the ways I abuse the English language.

Molly McLain, who's only had to listen to me talk about Chase Miller for a year. She has the patience of a saint.

And as always, my family fended for themselves while I wrote this book and deserve many hugs and kisses.

# ABOUT THE AUTHOR

Zoe York lives in London, Ontario with her young family. She's currently chugging Americanos, wiping sticky fingers, and dreaming of heroes in and out of uniform.

www.zoeyork.com